MAX REMY
SPY FORCE
BLUE'S
REVENGE
D.ABELA

OXFORD
UNIVERSITY PRESS

OXFORD

UNIVERSITY PRESS

Great Clarendon Street, Oxford OX2 6DP

Oxford University Press is a department of the University of Oxford.
It furthers the University's objective of excellence in research, scholarship, and
education by publishing worldwide in

Oxford   New York
Auckland   Cape Town   Dar es Salaam   Hong Kong   Karachi
Kuala Lumpur   Madrid   Melbourne   Mexico City   Nairobi
New Delhi   Shanghai   Taipei   Toronto

With offices in
Argentina   Austria   Brazil   Chile   Czech Republic   France   Greece
Guatemala   Hungary   Italy   Japan   Poland   Portugal   Singapore
South Korea   Switzerland   Thailand   Turkey   Ukraine   Vietnam

Oxford is a registered trade mark of Oxford University Press
in the UK and in certain other countries

First published 2004 by Random House Australia Pty Ltd,
Sydney, Australia. This edition published by arrangement
with Random House Australia.

First published in the UK in 2006

British Library Cataloguing in Publication Data

Data available

ISBN-13: 978-0-19-275423-3
ISBN-10: 0-19-275423-8

1 3 5 7 9 10 8 6 4 2

Typeset in Goudy by Palimpsest Book Production Limited,
Polmont, Stirlingshire

Printed in Great Britain by Cox & Wyman, Reading, Berkshire

For Phoebe, Olivia, Allie, and Tony

CHAPTER 1
A MOROCCAN MENACE

The midday sun burned down on the winding, narrow streets of Fez. Like an invisible blanket of fire, it scorched the air and ground, making it hard to move and even harder to breathe. A sluggish breeze, singed with heat, blew dry and stale into the sweating faces of shoppers and merchants alike, so that the haggling over carpets, jewellery, and finely crafted silverware lost the gusto of the early morning trade.

Max and Linden were in the Old Medina, an ancient walled part of the city crisscrossed by dusty, crooked alleys, at times no bigger than two outstretched arms. It was filled with covered bazaars, workshops, food stands, and restaurants as small as cupboards, all huddled together under the scorching North African sun.

Small clusters of robed people swished past, their feet kicking up the dirt of the alleyway. Young boys carrying trays with glasses of mint tea stopped and sold them to anyone who would listen. Carpet sellers sat on the steps of their small, crowded shops, their rugs and carpets dripping down the walls around them as they fanned themselves with newspapers or postcards.

'Think this looks any good?'

Linden picked up a red, tasselled fez from a

table in front of them and pushed it onto his tornado-style hair.

'The girls won't be able to hold themselves back,' Max said with a wisecracking smile.

Max and Linden were working undercover as tourists in Morocco. While they pretended to shop and sightsee, they were really trailing the movements of Levi Haddock, a tub-bellied ball of a man with no neck, googly eyes, and an unfortunate, death-inducing case of body odour.

Spy Force had been keeping an eye on Haddock for the past twelve months. He had been caught by the Moroccan police for a few minor misdemeanours, like evading import taxes and not keeping his camels properly tied up at night, but the police knew he was guilty of bigger crimes only they lacked the evidence to prove it.

Spy Force had used their wider contacts and internationally-trained agents to delve deeper into Haddock's activities and soon found he was implicated in several very crooked schemes. He'd laundered money through phoney dry-cleaning businesses in Berlin, smuggled uncut diamonds out of Saudi Arabia in tins of sardines, and had been responsible for acts of karaoke in Japan that, while not illegal, deserved to be listed as crimes.

It was now up to Max and Linden to find firm proof of Haddock's criminal activities and lead him to his capture.

They'd been spending their weekend with Max's Uncle Ben and Aunt Eleanor at their farm in Mindawarra when Spy Force contacted them about the mission. Steinberger, the Administration Manager of the Force, assured them that with their skills as spies, it would take no longer than twenty-four hours to bring Haddock in, leaving them plenty of time to be ready for school on Monday morning.

Max and Linden happily accepted the mission, partly for the excitement but also because it gave Max something to think about other than her mother's wedding, which had taken over their lives and was happening in only a few days.

Linden decided against the fez and took a mouthful from his water bottle, and just as his head tipped back, he saw him. The round-bellied man was standing on a veranda directly above them, stretching and yawning after his afternoon nap.

'Max, it's Haddock.'

But when Linden turned round, Max had walked to another stall and was haggling over the price of a large teapot.

'Max,' he whispered.

Haddock disappeared inside and the door closed behind him. Within minutes he was on the street, carrying a small suitcase and walking away from them.

Linden thought about the quickest way to get Max's attention and, even though he knew she wouldn't like it, raced over and grabbed her, making sure his hand was across her mouth. He ran with Max flung beside him, hoping her muffled protests wouldn't attract attention.

Then Haddock stopped.

Linden looked around quickly before pulling Max into the doorway of an antique shop and looking her in the eye.

'It's Haddock.' He took his hand away from her mouth.

'Haddock?' Max almost choked. 'What are we doing here? We should be after him!'

Linden sighed. 'Why didn't I think of that?'

Max peered out from the doorway to see Haddock sipping tea from one of the young sellers. 'We have to be discreet,' she cautioned, 'so don't do anything that's going to attract attention.'

But as she stepped out of the doorway, Max became entangled in a piece of rope strung from the roof, which was holding up a tangled cluster of silver pots and jugs.

'Uh-oh.' Linden watched as the pots fell towards them like a collapsing silver tent. He apologized briefly to the owner, who was standing in silent shock, and pulled Max outside, pushing her beneath a nearby stall that was covered with woven baskets and pointy leather slippers.

Max crouched guiltily beneath the curtained table, avoiding Linden's pointed stare and desperately hoping Haddock hadn't noticed the scene she'd caused.

'I've seen you be more discreet, you know.' Linden sneaked a look outside.

Haddock sipped the last of his tea, offering a scant look over his shoulder at the hand-waving owner and the sudden debris of antiques, before leaving coins on the boy's tea tray and walking away.

'Let's go.' Linden shot out from beneath the table and slowed into the casual stroll of a tourist shopping. Max was soon beside him as Haddock turned into an even narrower alley.

Linden slid down a wall opposite, keeping Haddock in sight. He took out a tatty, dog-eared book called *The Tourist Guide to Morocco*, which secretly concealed an Electronic Positioning Finder or EPF.

Haddock ducked his head slightly as he pushed aside a beaded curtain and stepped into a small, sand-coloured shop. Linden studied the EPF. 'It's the entrance to a jeweller.'

Max slid down beside him and winced at the fiery grill beside them, packed with smoking skewers of goat. Max's vegetarian nose still wasn't used to the many food stalls that lined the streets, all selling sizzling meat.

She took out her X-ray Spectrogram, a device that looked like a pocket computer game but was able to look through walls and inside buildings. For anyone who was watching, they were just two kids, taking an innocent break in the shade of a small street, playing games and reading books.

'What's he doing?' Linden turned a page of his guide, pretending to read.

Max looked at the grainy picture on the Spectrogram. 'He's talking to a large man with a beard who is wearing more jewellery than my mother.' Max adjusted the parameters of the Spectrogram to get a better view of where Haddock was. 'They're surrounded by lots of cupboards and glass cabinets filled with all sorts of jewellery.'

'Can you see any other rooms?'

'There's a door that leads to one with a sink and a small stove. Looks like a regular kitchen, though.' Max looked further and smiled. 'There's a secret passage concealed behind a wall rug and it's full of metal crates.'

'Can you get a read on what's in them?'

Max zeroed in on the contents of one of the boxes and programmed the Spectrogram to give her an object ID. 'It's doing it now . . . Hello there.'

'What's happening?'

'Mr Jewellery is showing Haddock inside the hidden room. He's opening a box and handing Haddock a small metallic cylinder. Haddock's looking at it closely. Now he's giving it back, along with his suitcase.'

'Which is full of cash,' Linden guessed.

Max watched as Mr Jewellery opened the case, revealing wads of notes. 'Bingo, Einstein.' Her screen lit up with the words:

ID Complete

She read from the screen. 'It's a detonator device for bombs. Highly sophisticated bombs that are capable of—'

A hand reached down from above and snatched the Spectrogram out of Max's hands. She looked up to see a huge robed man, smiling through crooked, yellow teeth. His bowl-sized hands crushed the device as if it was made of cardboard.

'Something tells me he's not happy to see us.' Linden closed his guidebook as the man dropped the useless chunk of ex-Spectrogram beside Max.

'Uh huh.' Max gulped.

The man then spoke into his sleeve, as if he was talking into a two-way radio.

Linden snatched his water bottle from his pocket and squirted it into the man's face. The man recoiled, giving them a few seconds to make a run for it. Linden darted into the crowd, with Max following close behind, just as Haddock came running from the jeweller's shop, his eyes ablaze, looking frantically around. He saw the young spies and bounded towards them.

The streets were beginning to fill again after the traditional midday sleep and Max and Linden dodged and wove between small children playing games, men carrying wooden carvings, and an old woman leading an overloaded donkey. They jumped over the hunched body of a young girl drawing in the sand and only just managed to limbo under a thick roll of carpet being carried by two small boys.

Haddock, for all his bulk, was still close on their tail.

'Down here.' Linden led Max down a dusty back alley. It twisted and turned at sharp angles.

They dived through a small archway lined with washing and almost collided with a man carrying a basket full of tomatoes. The man held his basket high and turned on his heels so he wouldn't lose his precious load, but his relief was short-lived when he was railroaded by Haddock's bulky frame tearing in behind them. The two men clashed and the tomatoes fountained into the air before raining down like paint-bombs. The owner began a stream of curses and wailing. Haddock merely snarled at him, wiped tomato goo off his face, and turned to see Max and Linden continue their flight.

'You won't escape me in here.'

He followed them up an old splintered ladder that led him onto the lip of what looked like a giant paintbox. These were the mudbrick pools of the tanneries. Deep round vats were filled with brilliant reds, oranges, and deep browns for dyeing leather. Surrounding them was a maze of wooden beams dripping with newly dyed animal skins.

'Could this place smell any worse?' Max took short, shallow breaths to minimize the strong-smelling odours that were itching her nose.

Max and Linden ran along the narrow rims. They sped past men with their robes wrapped around their waists like billowing shorts, their fingers and hands stained as they slushed the skins in and out of the coloured vats.

Linden turned round. 'Haddock's still following.' He gingerly pushed aside a large, dripping red skin, which slipped out of his hand and slapped into Max's face.

'Euwww.' She pushed away the bright red curtain, which left lines of red dye on her like a bad case of streaky sunburn. 'Mum's going to kill me if this stuff doesn't come off in time for the wedding. It washes off, right?'

Linden didn't have time to answer. Haddock was almost on top of them. 'Quick. This way.'

Max wiped dripping dye from her face as Linden headed off along a narrow ledge, but when they rounded a bend, they found themselves trapped in a dark and inescapable corner.

'That's enough of the games now, eh?' Haddock wheezed as he stumbled to a stop behind them.

Linden discreetly pressed a recorder button on

his watch before the two spies slowly turned to see their grinning pursuer. Haddock took a hanky from inside his robe and dabbed his sweating brow and cheeks. What he took out next, though, was less innocent. He pushed back his robe and revealed a long metal sheath hanging from a leather belt.

'Let me introduce you to my sword. It has been in my family for three hundred years and has been victorious in many battles against intruders.'

The sound of the sword being torn from the sheath echoed around them. He ran the ancient blade across his palm and drew instant blood.

'Just to let you know how good it is.'

'Oh, we believe you.' Max wasn't sure if it was the airless heat, the smells of the tannery, or the drips of blood falling from Haddock's hand that were making her feel woozy. 'What do you want with the detonators?'

Haddock eyed her hungrily. 'As if I would tell a couple of puny brats.'

He laughed as he raised the blade above his head, both hands gripping the ornamental handle, and took one step towards them. Max and Linden looked down at the large dyed skin he now stood on and only just held back two victorious smiles.

Haddock gathered a lungful of air to prepare for

his strike, but as he was about to bring the blade down, ropes tied to each corner of the animal skin beneath him jerked upwards towards a wooden pulley, knocking the sword from his hands and lifting him into the air like a sack of cargo being loaded onto a ship.

'Now, Haddock, tell us about the detonators,' Max ordered.

'Never!' Haddock's reply was muffled but furious.

Three robed Spy Force agents, who were the obvious creators of the smelly trap, appeared before Max and Linden. A fourth stood beside them, surveying their handiwork.

'I'm Agent Madison. Well done. You followed the coordinates to the capture site precisely. Did you get the proof?'

'We caught him on the X-ray Spectrogram buying detonators. Now we just need to persuade him to tell us why.'

Agent Madison smiled. 'Certainly.'

She nodded to the three other agents, who swung the pulley, loosened the ropes, and sent Haddock plunging into a deep red vat. The pool bubbled into life until, after a few seconds, they lifted the sack out with spluttering sound effects.

'Now will you tell us?' Max asked politely.

'No! You rotten, despicable, camel-smelling—'

Max gave the nod for another dunking.

This time, Haddock's swim was a little longer, and when his sack was pulled upwards, his gasping cough was accompanied by a promise to co-operate.

'OK! OK! The detonators were going to be used to remove a few obstacles in the way of some of my business dealings.'

'I think that'll be enough for now. We can get the rest later,' Agent Madison said. 'Do you have the location of where the deal took place?'

Linden handed over his guidebook with the concealed EPF. 'It's in here.'

Madison was impressed. 'Excellent work. As usual.'

The agents lowered the bag to the ground. Haddock emerged looking like an overcooked tomato and smelling like a garbage truck at the end of a long night of pick-ups. The agents cuffed his hands and led him away to his new home, provided courtesy of the Moroccan police.

Linden turned to Max as they walked away from the tanneries. 'I guess we can chalk up another victory.'

'I guess we can.' Max smiled before she was

struck by a different thought. 'It's not the same now that Blue is in prison.* Don't get me wrong, I like it this way, but even though he's behind bars, I keep worrying that he's thinking up a new plan to out-evil his last scheme.'

'I don't think we have to worry about Blue. By the time he gets out of prison we'll be sitting in a retirement home for old has-been scientists.' Linden gave a wicked grin. 'Time for a sizzling skewer of goat, eh?'

Max screwed up her nose as Linden nudged her in the shoulder and laughed.

It did feel good that Blue was locked away, but Max had fought him enough times to know he never gave up a fight easily, and when it came to Spy Force, the fight was a long way from over.

* See Max Remy Spy Force: The Amazon Experiment

CHAPTER 2

A HIGH SECURITY VISIT AND A SPECIAL GIFT

Far from the dust and alleyways of Morocco, a small, hunched woman shrouded in a long, black shawl was led down murkily lit corridors into a series of grey, echoing rooms. Security was tight. Cameras fixed to the roof and walls whirred in the direction of any moving person or object. The guard beside the old woman held one hand over his gun and rested the other on the baton that swung in a holster at his side. He was also equipped with a Stinger, a small, electrically charged device that delivered a jolting current into the nervous system, rendering a person immobile for hours.

The woman's frail, careful steps seemed childlike next to the long stride of the guard in his metal-capped boots. But even though she appeared harmless, the woman was processed like any other visitor to Blacksea Penitentiary, an international prison perched on the rocky, barren landscape of Coffin Island. Lapped by seas that even in the midday sun looked as if they had been stained by an oil spill, the Penitentiary held the record for being the only modern prison in the world that hadn't had one escape in its wretched twenty-year history. If a prisoner was to break through its security, they would be left with the choice of jumping into the high swell of the ocean and swimming fifty kilometres through shark-speckled seas to the shore, or turning back and begging the guards to let them in to escape the treeless island's cruel sun and forlorn nights.

The old woman had been fingerprinted, had handed over her dental records, and her face had been scanned and checked against an international database of criminals. She was then brought to a table with a harsh fluorescent light overhead. Beside the table was a white-coated technician and a tall, cylindrical 360-degree X-ray machine.

'Empty your pockets,' the guard snarled.

The old woman delved into her many layers of clothing and pulled out a crumpled handkerchief, keys, a few coins, a packet of mints, and a thick metal disc. The last item she held before her. 'It is a fob watch,' she explained.

The guard sniffed and took the watch. He flicked open the catch and stared at its careful craftsmanship, finely carved hands, and gold-inlaid date of 1842. On the back was an inscription:

Even at Sea you will Never be far from Home

The woman stared pleadingly at the guard, her ice-blue eyes shining with tears. 'It belonged to his grandfather and his grandfather before him. It has seen them through many hard times and I hope it will help my grandson through his.'

The guard remained unmoved.

'Please. I am an old woman.' She wrung her hands at the possibility that her gift would not be allowed through.

The guard grunted and handed the watch to the technician, who opened a hatch in the X-ray machine and slid it inside. He closed the small door and pressed a series of buttons on a remote control. A low-level humming could be heard, and a picture of the inside of the watch appeared on a screen embedded into the machine. After a few seconds, a soft 'ping' sounded. The technician removed the watch and handed it back to the guard. 'It's clean.'

'Step up here,' the guard ordered.

It was now the old woman's turn for an X-ray. She exhaled a gasping wheeze as she lifted her multi-layered skirts, stepped into the machine, and was told to stand as still as she could. She looked uneasy as a low-level hum reverberated around her. After a few minutes, the technician gave a nod and she was allowed to step out.

'The visitors' room is through that door.' The guard handed over the woman's possessions and the two men watched as she ambled away.

'I wasn't really expecting Grandma to be carrying any sub-machine guns.' The technician sniffed back a laugh.

'Gotta be done.' The guard's expression was cold and hard.

Their voices echoed behind the woman as she stopped before a reinforced metal door. It opened with a click and whining hum, and the woman trudged into a long, glass tube suspended over the frenzied waves of Coffin Island's western edge. She flinched as a spear of lightning cracked overhead and sizzled into the ocean. She pulled her shawl around her shoulders and shuffled quickly along the tube.

At the end was a small glass-domed room which allowed a full view of the restless expanse of stormy ocean. In the centre of the room was a table and two chairs. Another lightning strike split the sky as the old woman slumped into a chair with a weary sigh. Her eyes flicked around the room and she saw tiny cameras fixed into the dome's walls, watching her every move.

It was then she heard the footsteps, as the guard led in the prisoner.

It was Mr Blue.

'Grandma!'

The woman held out her arms for a hug but the guard quickly stepped between them and led Blue to the chair on the opposite side of the table. He then took up a position in the middle, watching over both of them.

'You look thin.' The woman's voice croaked with sadness.

'The budget for the kitchen doesn't extend to buying real food.' Blue shot the guard a sharp glare. 'How is everyone?'

'Fine. Looking forward to the day you come home.'

Blue's head sank forward. 'That won't be for a long time yet.'

Another splinter of lightning broke through the blackness, followed by a rumble of thunder.

The woman sniffed into a handkerchief. 'It's not right that you are here.'

'We all have to face justice, Grandma.' He reached out to touch her hand but the guard took a menacing step forward so he stopped. 'Are they keeping busy?'

The old woman sighed. 'You know how they are, always working.'

Blue smiled.

'Apart from you being here, everything is in its place.' Her face, concealed by the hanky, was lit up by more lightning as she gave Blue a brief, pointed look.

The guard looked at his watch. 'Time's up.'

'So soon?'

The woman stood up and reached into her shawl. 'Your grandfather wants you to have this. To get you through this difficult time.'

Blue took the watch and his eyes were lit by a brief glint of excitement. He then watched as his grandmother was led down the sea-sprayed glass tube. The horizon was electrified by blue-white javelins of lightning. She would be taken through a series of exit screening rooms, before being delivered to a waiting chopper that would take her to the mainland.

After Blue had been escorted back to his cell, he listened as the reinforced double doors were locked behind him and the clack of the guards' metal-capped boots ricocheted off the stone walls as they moved away.

He sat on his grey prison blanket and held the watch before him, turning it in the dim glow of the overhead light. It looked worn from years of use, scratched and dented by who-knows-what unforeseen event or, and here he had to smile, 'difficult time'.

He turned the watch and read aloud the inscribed message. 'Even at sea you will never be far from home . . . How right you will be,' he predicted.

Leaning forward, he reached under his bed and removed a small jeweller's screwdriver from inside the mattress. Holding it steady, he undid a tiny bolt on the back of the watch and opened the metal covering.

A small gasp escaped from Blue as he marvelled at what he was seeing. He was holding a genuine watch, but what it concealed within its mechanisms was the real gift.

Replacing the miniature screwdriver inside the mattress, he got up from his bed and held the metal device in front of him. Arms outstretched, Blue stood perfectly still, the opened inside of the watch pointed directly at his eyes. He flinched as a loud bellow of thunder rattled the glass of his window and sent a bolt of lightning so bright he had to blink the sting of it away.

He straightened up and threw his head back in a confident flick.

'Now let's see what all our years of hard work have earned us.'

Blue's thumb rested on the winding mechanism at the top of the watch. With a deep breath and a sharp grin, he pressed down hard.

A green-tinged beam of light poured out of the watch and struck Blue with a steamrolling force. It entered his eyes and created a sizzling outline that crept around and down his body. He held his arms out before him, trying not to break the connection between his eyes and the powerful beam.

Blue held firm as the frenzy of the storm outside filled the room with jolts of lightning and unearthly, quaking thunder.

The pressure of the watch's crackling process was beginning to send spasms of pain through Blue's body, but as the light passed below his knees he clenched his teeth, refusing to give up.

When the light reached his feet, it went out, as if it was a torch that had been suddenly switched off. With a deep, stabilizing breath and a smile dripping with anticipation, Blue prepared to see the results of his night's work.

A dark figure stepped out from the shadows of his cell. Blue's breath caught in his chest as he witnessed a spectacle modern science had until now only dreamt of.

'Even after a bout in prison you still look good.'

Blue leant in close to the figure, his nose a hair's-breadth away from the chiselled features of this fine, new face. He stood back, smirking beneath a raised eyebrow.

He was standing before an identical replica of himself.

'Much quicker than cloning, don't you think? And definitely better-looking.'

Blue looked up as a pair of gloved hands suddenly appeared at the window and gripped onto the bars.

'Ah, Sorenson, right on time.' Blue opened the window and took what looked like a leather wristwatch from the gloved fingers. He folded it around his wrist, pressed the clasp, and adjusted the settings.

'The energy from this little device should send out interference waves that will block any security system in the world,' he explained to his double. 'I'll be as good as invisible.'

The two Blues watched as Sorenson's gloved hands suctioned thin, metal rods onto the window bars.

'And those,' Blue continued, 'are Particle Distortion Devices that are able to change the basic make-up of any metal.'

They watched as a red light glowed from the end of each device. After a few seconds, a short beep was heard. Sorenson then held on to the bars and bent them as easily as sticks of liquorice.

'It's time for me to leave. Do you mind?'

Blue's double interlaced his hands together, forming a stirrup. Blue stepped into them, lifted himself up and climbed out of the window so he stood beside Sorenson on the mossy stone wall of the prison exterior.

'You are worth every one of the many pennies I am paying you.'

Sorenson nodded before replacing the metal bars and bending them back to their original shape. He then removed the Particle Distortion Devices, reinforcing the bars to their original strength.

Blue turned towards the face peering out of what had been his cell. 'You be good now.'

He followed Sorenson over the scrubby grass of the prison yard to the edge of the cliff. Sweeping searchlights lit the ground in wide arcs. At times the two men were caught in the full glare of the lights. 'Undetectable!' Blue exclaimed. 'The fools thought they could keep me here!'

At the cliff's edge the wind erupted around them, piercing them with cold sprays of seawater churned up by the storm.

Just out of sight, beneath the overhang of the cliff edge, a mini helicopter was firmly anchored to the cliff. The two men climbed down the rocky slope with the aid of a rope and, moving carefully, scrambled inside the craft. Sorenson then released the anchors, started the engine and they were away.

'So long, Blacksea. Sorry I can't stay longer, but I have some important business to attend to.' Blue sniggered in delight. 'And a spy agency to bring down.'

The hovering aircraft swayed over the rising waves and within seconds had disappeared into the inky clutches of the night.

Not far away, another chopper struggled to navigate the slamming winds as one of its passengers watched Blacksea disappear into the mist. She sank into her shawl as a flash of lightning spilled onto her face. Ms Peckham let loose a quiet, victorious laugh. 'We shall see you soon, sir.'

CHAPTER 3
SILVER MEDALLIONS AND AN ENEMY SIGHTING

'Looks like you two have come to an end!'

Max and Linden stared at Harrison, not knowing what to do or say. This wasn't the welcome home they'd expected.

Steinberger looked away awkwardly.

A silence lined with anticipation poured into the room.

'Looks like you two have . . .' Seconds passed. '. . . *done it again* is what I meant to say.'

Harrison, the Chief of Spy Force, breathed a disappointed sigh. He was known for his occasional mismanaging of words. In fact, whole sentences sometimes escaped from his lips making no sense at all. He looked down at his sprained wrist, which was cradled in a sling due to an accident with a tea trolley, a dish of cream buns, and a rather quickly revolving door.

Max looked at Harrison's dejected face. She liked his way with words. Even though they weren't quite the right words at times, she'd miss it if he changed.

'Not to worry, sir.' Steinberger, as usual, was by his chief's side. 'For now, there's something we have to say to our two youngest spies.'

'Yes. Yes, of course.' Harrison lifted two silver medallions from his desk drawer. They were stamped with the Spy Force insignia and the following inscription:

May the Force be with You

'And this is how we'd like to do it. Steinberger?'

Steinberger rotated a small white knob on the wall and the lights dimmed. A button clicked and the sound of a brass band piped up in full swing. A spotlight lit up the proud and now composed face of Harrison, who held the medallions before him.

'Max Remy and Linden Franklin, as Chief of Spy Force it is my pleasure to award you these medals for the successful completion of your fifth mission at the Force.'

The volume of the brass band increased, accompanied by the splatter of excited applause. Max gave Linden a triumphant smile. Before joining Spy Force she had been convinced she was no good at anything, but standing here beside

Linden, she knew they made a great spy team.

'You have both shown a level of courage and skill that is extraordinary. You've mastered Spy Force equipment, expertly followed mission briefs, and even overcome a certain tendency to . . .' Harrison levelled a gentle eye at Max. '. . . anger.'

Max bit her lip, knowing her temper wasn't her best quality.

'We are proud to have you on our team.'

Harrison leant forward and carefully placed the medallions around Max's and Linden's necks. The band crescendoed into a brassy explosion of trumpets, drums, tubas, and cymbals. The lights flickered in a celebratory frenzy and small glittering pieces of tinsel fell around them.

Without warning, the music stopped and a mumbled 'ooph' and clatter of metal was heard as Steinberger stumbled to the light switch and restored the room to a Spy Force office once again.

'Excrement!'

There was another strained silence. The proud look drained from Harrison's face with his latest word blunder. 'I mean,' he lilted, '*excellent*, of course.'

He sat down with a heavy thud.

Max was eager to see his smile return. 'It's an

honour working with you, sir.' She grinned so widely her cheeks started to hurt.

'I think so too.' Linden blew a strand of hair from his eyes and let loose one of his smiles. 'We wouldn't want to work for anyone else.'

A loud sniff sounded behind them. 'Me too, sir.' Steinberger was doing very badly at hiding an urge to cry. 'The agency would be a mere shadow of itself if it wasn't for your leadership.'

Now it was Harrison's turn to get all teary.

'Permission to hug you, sir?' Steinberger asked.

'Permission granted,' Harrison replied.

The two men moved in and, with Harrison's bandaged arm nestled between them, they hugged firmly, sniffing into each other's shoulders.

Max shuffled awkwardly. 'I think we'd better leave.'

The two men untangled themselves. 'Yes. Of course.' Harrison took out a hanky with his one good arm and blew his nose. 'Sorry about that. Things have been a little . . . emotional . . . since the sleeping sickness almost, well . . . almost saw our end.'*

Harrison gathered up a smile. 'But you're right.

* See *Max Remy Spy Force: The Amazon Experiment*

It's time for school. Sleek is waiting in the VART to take you there.'

Max was relieved the two men had pulled themselves together. She wasn't good at displays of emotion and wasn't planning on changing that any time soon.

Harrison and Steinberger escorted Max and Linden to the Vehicular All-Response Tower, the hangar where all the Spy Force vehicles were kept. Once inside, Max stopped to say a final goodbye. 'Sir? What about Blue?'

'Blue is safely behind bars.'

But Max knew he was holding back and gave him a look that told him she wasn't going anywhere until she heard more.

'Sir, we can handle whatever you have to say.'

Harrison knew the boundless reaches of Blue's brilliant mind and his capacity for evil. Even though he was safely locked away, they would be foolish to underestimate his intelligence or his determination to get what he wanted. Harrison reluctantly continued.

'After your mission in the Amazon, I believe Blue will not rest until he has had a chance to . . .' He paused, searching for the right words. 'To get his revenge.'

This last sentence fell between them like a wrecking ball cracking against steel.

'Do you know if he is planning anything?' Linden held his silver medallion close to his chest.

'No, but he is being held in a maximum security prison and the second he breaks even the smallest rule, we will be immediately notified.'

The squeal of a loudspeaker system shot out above them.

'This is your captain speaking. Express flight to Sydney courtesy of the Invisible Jet is ready for take-off. Please board the plane, take your seats and settle in for a new and improved ride through the skies.'

'Is the Invisible Jet fixed?' Linden looked behind him at where the jet would be if he could see it.

'The crash landing in the Amazon gave it quite a nasty makeover but Sleek has been working night and day to repair it.' Steinberger proudly gazed at the seemingly empty space where the jet was parked. 'He has outdone himself this time. It is faster, more fuel efficient, and quieter on take-offs and landings. But I'm afraid there's still the Automatic People Sanitizer.'

Max groaned. The Sanitizer was a balloon-walled room at the entrance of the jet that acted as an all-over human vacuum cleaner. After its passengers were jostled, bounced, and cleaned, it felt as if they'd had their brains sucked out. Or at least that's how Max felt.

'We thought after your mission in Morocco you'd be grateful for the jet's hearty meals and time to rest before school,' Harrison explained.

Linden's eyes drifted dreamily. 'Food. Yeah. That'd be great.'

The loudspeaker squealed again. 'This is your captain speaking, take-off is in thirty seconds.'

'Gotta run.' Max and Linden caught sight of the interior of the plane through the invisible door and leapt inside. After the usual brain-sucking jostling of the Sanitizer, they hurriedly took their seats just in time for Roger the cabin-hand to lock the doors and take his own seat. The jet then lifted to hovering and shot like a catapult out of the VART and into the skies above London.

Linden immediately opened the Digital Think Amajig that was nestled in the armrest of his chair and ordered a hamburger with the lot, a chocolate milkshake, and a bowl of chips.

Max doubted even Linden could eat that much. 'You sure that's going to be enough?'

Linden looked concerned. 'You're right.' He

added a side order of fish fingers. 'That should do it.'

Max smiled until Harrison's words came back to her.

'Linden, do you think Blue is planning his revenge?'

Linden looked down the aisle, eager to spot Roger bringing his food. 'He's under maximum security. I don't think he can plan much.' He noticed Max hadn't ordered her meal.

'Aren't you going to eat anything?'

'Maybe later.' Max looked out of the window. She had suddenly remembered that her mother's wedding was at the weekend, a thought even more unsettling than Harrison's suspicions of Blue.

Later, as Linden finished the last mouthful of hamburger, the jet slowed down and Sleek's voice floated over their heads.

'This is your captain again. We will shortly be arriving in Sydney before heading west to Mindawarra. Please make sure your tray tables are stowed and your seats are in an upright position. I hope you enjoyed your trip and choose to fly again with Sleek.'

'He's in a good mood.' Max had never heard Sleek sounding so happy.

'Must be relieved to have the jet back together.'

The windows filled with the deep blue expanse of Sydney Harbour that lit up with the morning sun so that it looked like a dappled bed of diamonds. Lush green parks and wild bushland nestled snugly around its shores. Boats and ferries jostled on its surface and a passenger ship sailed under the world's most famous coathanger, the Harbour Bridge.

The jet turned inland and slowed down to a hovering standstill, just above a large tree in a park near Max's school.

'See you at the weekend?' Linden asked carefully.

'Sure.' Max tried to sound excited. Even though there was very little chance of the wedding being anything but a total nightmare, at least with Eleanor, Ben, and Linden there, she might just make it through alive. 'Well done on another successful mission, partner,' she added.

'Couldn't have done it without you, chief.'

'I know.' Max spun around and pressed the exit button. The door opened upwards and she walked past the deflated Sanitizer walls to the edge of the hovering jet. After slipping on her super-grip gloves, she grabbed hold of an Abseiler rope that was attached to the roof.

Max took a deep breath before lowering herself into the thick camouflage of the tree. Seconds later, she landed safely on the ground.

She looked up and watched as the Abseiler rope moved upwards and disappeared. The top of the tree swayed slightly as if a gust of wind had stirred it, and Max knew the jet had turned and was headed to Mindawarra.

After she'd brushed herself down and removed her gloves, she flipped open the top of her red chrome Spy Force watch and smiled. There was just enough time to make it to school before the bell rang. She'd been late a few times during last term. So far she'd managed to keep Principal Peasers off her back with faked notes, believable-sounding excuses, and Oscar award-winning limping on 'sprained' ankles, but she knew if she pushed it any further, her luck would run out.

But when she came out from behind the tree, she saw something she hadn't expected.

Toby.

He was sitting on a bench only metres away.

Her heart did a weird flip as if someone had

tossed it like pizza dough. Why was he here? And alone? And why did he look so sad?

It was then he looked up and instantly flashed her a wide grin.

Max faked a casual semi-smile that she suspected looked anything but casual.

She was about to give Toby a brief wave and keep walking, but his smile faded and there was something about his look that wouldn't let her leave.

'Great,' she mumbled. Even though Toby had made her life a misery from the day they'd met, she couldn't walk away.

'Out walking with all your friends?' Toby asked when she stood before him.

Max raised one eyebrow. 'No, I thought I'd try walking with all *your* friends instead.'

Toby smiled. There weren't many people who could give back like Max could.

'At least this way you're finally the smartest one in the group.'

Max winced through a smile. Toby was obviously fine. Why did she even bother stopping? 'Yes, and now I have to get to school so I can become even smarter.'

When she turned to leave, she again saw his face

fall. Something was up. She could feel it. And why was he just sitting here when they were late already? Then she did something she couldn't explain.

'Do you want to walk to school together?'

What? Max's brain silently asked her mouth. Walk to school together? Was she crazy? What was it about this boy that made her act all weird?

Toby looked as if he was going to accept. Max held her breath. Escaping from sword-wielding criminals in Morocco suddenly seemed easy compared to spending whole minutes side by side with Mr Popularity, where she'd only end up finding a new way to make a fool of herself.

As if he'd guessed her thoughts, Toby stood up and threw his bag over his shoulder.

'Nah. I've gotta do something first. And I . . .'

He looked as if he wanted to say something else but stopped himself and changed the subject. 'What are you doing walking this way anyway? You live the other way.'

Max froze. 'I . . . um. It's just that . . . I wanted to have a walk before school.'

Good one, Max silently grumbled. Very convincing.

'Oh.' Toby answered as if he didn't believe her. 'Me too.'

Max stared after him as he walked away, his feet shuffling along the gravel path. She was relieved he had refused to walk with her, but now she felt bad again. Toby could do that. Make her swing from not wanting to have anything to do with him to feeling bad about being mean to him, even though he was the expert when it came to being mean.

Either way, there was no time to think about it. She pulled her bag against her chest. If she ran all the way to school she might just be able to slip into assembly without being noticed.

CHAPTER 4
COW MANURE BRAINS AND A SNEAKY DEAL

'Lovely day, Max.'

No, no, no, Max thought. Not Peasers. The principal of love and happiness. The queen of mush. Where did she come from?

'Ahh, Peasers . . . I mean, Ms Peasley.'

Why was it Max could thwart criminals all over the world, make it through the Amazon Jungle and escape from a Nightmare Vortex, but she couldn't sneak into school five minutes after the bell? She had to divert Peasers's attention from her being late.

'Aren't you . . .' Peasers lifted her wrist to look at her watch. Max had to think fast.

'I don't know if you get told often enough, Ms Peasley, but I just wanted to say how excellent it is to have you as our principal.'

'Oh, thank you, Max.' Ms Peasley blushed beneath her pink eye shadow and lowered her hand. 'That's very kind.'

Good start, Max thought to herself. Keep it up.

'And that concert last Friday? We all owe its success to the direction we get from you. As everyone knows, that kind of talent radiates down from above.'

Peasers adjusted her hair, which was overloaded with frangipanis. 'It is sweet of you to say, Max, but the students worked very hard.'

Max had on her sweetest smile. Now it was time to go in for the kill.

'But, Ms Peasley, a good performance comes from love, and it is your guidance that has brought us that love.'

For a terrible second, Max thought Peasers was going to hug her.

'Yes, well, I always say a school that sings together grows together. Why, just last week I was at a seminar on fostering a harmonious playground and I—'

'Actually, Ms Peasley, I need to go or I'll be late for class.'

'Of course. It's always a pleasure talking to such a conscientious student.'

Max turned and walked down the corridor. She never thought she'd ever be this happy to go to maths.

After Max had explained she was late because she was talking to the principal, she sat down, took out her books and looked around. There was the same old Monday morning sleepiness over everyone's face, but Max noticed something else. Toby was missing. He hadn't made it to class. Maybe he had got caught up in whatever it was he had to do. Or maybe he was in trouble. She couldn't get his sad face out of her head, and the memory of those seconds when she knew he'd wanted to say something but didn't.

Something was wrong. She wasn't sure what or, more importantly, why she even cared. Mostly Toby did all he could to prove he had an oversupply of annoying genes, but there was also their mission in Hollywood he'd sneaked on to where he actually seemed halfway decent.* Even though Spy Force had erased his memory of the mission, something had changed between them. Something Max wasn't comfortable with at all.

At recess, she found herself standing in the middle of the playground like a spindly tree in need of watering.

'Why am I doing this?' she muttered out loud.

She walked over to Toby's friends, who were dividing up food from what looked like a post-tuckshop frenzy. As a firm rule of survival, Max never approached these guys, but when she did, it gave her the feeling of being thrown to a hungry pack of lions. Lions, of course, are much better-looking.

'Any of you guys seen Toby?'

* See *Max Remy Spy Force: The Hollywood Mission*

They stopped and stared, small glimmers of excitement replacing their scavenging scowls. Suddenly the possibility of a Max session was more exciting than chocolate and crisps.

'Why do you want to know were Toby is?' Josh was always the acting leader when Toby was away.

Max gave Josh a withering stare. She knew this had been a bad idea. 'I just want to know if you've seen him.'

'Maybe she wants to kiss him?' This was Zack. If you gave Zack and a monkey a maths test, they'd get the same results.

'Yeah. Yeah. Kiss him,' they all chorused, and then broke into hyena-like laughing. Max tried to stay calm.

'I need to tell him something.'

They weren't listening. Toby's friends never did. They loved the sound of their own voices too much to listen to anyone else.

'Maybe she wants to be his girlfriend.' It was Zack again.

An angry shiver rattled through Max's bones. She could feel her temper curdling into a bitter word-fest she wasn't going to be able to stop.

Josh had this slimy smile that Max wanted to plaster with mud. 'Or maybe she wants to marry him?'

That was it. Max took a deep breath and narrowed her eyes into two threatening slits. 'And maybe you've got cow manure for brains.'

'Ooooh!' They hooted like excited owls, happy that Max had taken the bait.

'And maybe you . . .' Josh began but Max walked away, trying to block out their insults, as they pretended to spray the air for lovesick germs and sang songs about Max and Toby sitting in trees kissing. She could have stayed and fought it out but she had other things to worry about. Like Toby, facing an English exam she hadn't studied for, and, the biggest worry, her mother's wedding.

She was heading for a seat as far away from Toby's gang as possible when Sasha, Georgie, and Grace spilled out of the corridor and turned towards her.

'Tell me they're not heading straight for me?' Max asked no one in particular.

She focused on the blue bread sandwich with pink cucumber filling and the carrot and honey hash brown that Irene had made for her lunch, hoping everything else would disappear.

It didn't.

The three girls stood in front of Max like overexcited puppies. They always wore the right clothes, got the right marks and had parents who looked as if they'd stepped out of a shampoo ad.

What did I do to deserve the way this day is turning out? Max thought as she bit into her sandwich.

'Max! Max! Is it true?'

In any other playground this might have been just another day at school, but these girls never spoke to Max, and in fact, until now, Max hadn't known they even knew her name. Either way, she was in no mood to start making friends with them today.

'Is what true?'

'You know!' Grace was short and had this high-pitched voice that could have cracked glass.

'Um.' Max prepared to take another bite of her sandwich. 'No, I don't.'

Sasha took over. She was cooler and more in control of her screech factor than Grace. 'That your mum is marrying Doctor Shannon?'

Dr Rex Shannon was Aidan's soap character's name. He played a psychologist and even had his own doll made in his image. And yes, despite how Max felt about it, he was marrying her mum. She tried to think of what to do next, of how she could make them go away. Then she had it.

Outright denial.

'Yeah right,' she scoffed, taking a bright red muffin from her lunchbox.

'Well, what's this?' Georgie flicked a magazine in Max's face and there, on the cover, was a picture of her mother and Dr Shannon posing in wedded bliss. Max swallowed to try to keep her lunch from flying out of her reeling stomach.

'I . . . I . . .'

When had this happened? Why hadn't she been told? Why was she always the last person to know anything her mother did?

'You mean your own mum didn't tell you she was getting married?' Georgie's eyebrows flew up so high they almost rocketed off her forehead. 'You have one strange family, Max Remy.'

They then walked away, swooning over how gorgeous Dr Shannon was and what they'd give to be his new stepdaughter.

Max stared at her muffin and lost her appetite for the second time that day. She put it back in her lunchbox and pushed hard on the lid. The bell was about to go so she slowly made her way past clutches of whispering students towards class.

Until she was slapped with her next idea.

'Georgie! Wait for me.'

The three princesses turned round with a confused, why-is-Max-talking-to-us look on their faces.

'How would you like Doctor Shannon's autograph?'

Grace squealed yes but Georgie simply stared at Max. She'd learnt early in life that whenever she was offered anything, there was always room to increase the offer to something better. 'On a photo?'

'Sure.' Max guessed this was possible, considering how much Aidan enjoyed pictures of himself.

'What do you want in return?'

'I need Toby's home number. Do you think you can get it?'

Georgie's mum worked in the school office, where Georgie spent most of her time after school trying to look important.

'Why do you want Toby's number?'

'If you want the autograph, you won't ask.'

Max could see this was torture for Georgie, who lived for gossip, but she wanted the signature more, so she gave in.

'I could do it in my sleep.' She eyed off the office with a slowly rising smile. 'Give me five minutes.'

Max, Grace, and Sasha watched through the office window as Georgie went into action. She held her hand against her forehead and almost fainted. Her mother helped her to a seat while she disappeared in search of a cold pack.

Max was impressed.

The instant her mum left the room, Georgie was on the computer, operating the student database as if she did it every day.

'She's obviously done this before,' Max guessed.

'Oh, lots of times.' Sasha watched in admiration.

Georgie wrote on a piece of paper and moved back to her chair just as her mother re-entered the room. None of the girls were surprised to see Georgie suddenly feeling better, and within thirty seconds she was standing next to them with the number.

Georgie handed it over. 'I expect the autograph by the end of the week.'

'Sure. Thanks.'

'Oh, and Max? Don't think because of this you need to start talking to us.'

Max was relieved they were thinking the same thing. 'Fine by me.'

As they walked away, the bell chimed for class. Max picked up her bag and folded the number into her pocket, frowning. She'd face the English test now and work out later how she was actually going to use the number without sounding like a complete idiot. Her life was sometimes very strange, and today was proving no different.

CHAPTER 5
THE BIG DAY

This was not their usual assignment.

Max looked at her watch again and wondered what she was doing here. She was a good agent, one of Spy Force's best, yet here she was nestled behind a blackberry bush playing babysitter to a spoilt rich kid.

'Ow!' Her finger sprang into her mouth. 'If I get stabbed one more time by a thorn, I'm going to sink the next time I go swimming.'

Linden smirked and looked away, deciding it was best not to answer. Max's mood was nosediving with each thorny scratch and even if he'd tried to sympathize, he knew he would only make it worse.

The kid they were guarding was Tobias Reardon, the son of an important foreign minister visiting England to discuss a peace plan aimed at settling decades of Middle East conflict. Many held high hopes for its success, but it was so controversial, the government feared opponents of the plan would do anything they could to ruin the talks. Even kidnap family. And because Tobias had an unfortunate habit of disappearing to explore his new surroundings, Max and Linden were put on assignment to make sure he didn't disappear for good.

With his miniature, high-powered binoculars, Linden peered into the Safe House Tobias and his family had been placed in. Tobias was reading, while his mother sat at her computer. Nothing suspicious. Nothing out of the ordinary.

The house was an unassuming, three-storey London terrace that sat at the edge of a small green square speckled with benches, trees, and neatly swept paths. The sun shone, birds tweeted, old couples strolled, and Max counted the wasted minutes of her life that might as well have been flushed down the toilet.

'If I'd wanted an assignment this exciting, I could have asked to have my brain removed and sent to Siberia.'

'I hear it's a nice place.' Sometimes Linden couldn't help himself. He was right, though. Answering didn't help Max's mood.

'Is that right? Well . . .'

'Hold on, Max.' Linden refocused his binoculars and flinched at what he saw. 'He's gone.'

The words sat in the air between them like a bad smell.

'Gone?'

'He must have slipped out.'

When Harrison had given them the mission, he told them that if anything happened to Tobias the security of the whole country, even the world, would be in terrible danger.

Then Linden spied something else. 'That car. Look.' A black saloon with tinted windows was parked near Tobias's house.

'And I'll bet that's the owner.'

Linden pointed towards a tracksuited man sitting on a park bench reading a newspaper. Max and Linden each pulled a silver pen from their pocket. They were designed by Quimby, Spy Force's head inventor, and contained darts that were guaranteed to put a person to sleep in seconds.

'We'll use these to immobilize Tobias and get him to the Spy Force vehicle.' Max took a brief look at the ice-cream van that was parked in front of them. It might have looked slow, but beneath the old-fashioned exterior was a super-fast car capable of speeds of up to 240 kilometres per hour.

'If we're quick, we can get to Tobias before he's taken on a joyride he may never return from.' Linden frowned. 'If we can find him . . .'

'There he is.' Max spied their young charge carefully creeping along the side of the house, but then her breath caught in her throat. 'Toby?' What was he doing here? He was in danger. Max had to save him.

But as they were about to leap out from behind the blackberry bush, the doors of the saloon burst open and two men leapt out, grabbed Tobias, and dragged him inside.

'The man with the baseball cap was a decoy,' Linden realized angrily. 'Let's go!'

The two spies ran to the ice-cream truck, and just as they jumped in, Max saw Toby's sad face peering out of the rear window of the black car. Seconds later, he was gone.

Max gulped down a rising lump of fear as she started the truck. They had to rescue Toby or the world was doomed to chaos, to madness, to unspeakable horrors, to—

'What are you still doing in bed?' The shrieking cry jolted Max from her nightmare so that she slammed her face into her wooden bedhead.

Her thoughts raced in circles as she tried to focus on what was happening and who the white-gowned person at her door was, with hair swept into a congealed foam pile, face plastered with thick green goo, and screaming like a wounded banshee.

'I woke you up an hour ago. Why are you still asleep? We won't get there at all at this rate!'

Then she realized. It was her mother. Max had

been woken up earlier, but she must have fallen back to sleep. And on the day of the wedding!

'I'll make sure she gets up this time.' Linden sneaked under the arm of Max's mother's fluffy white dressing-gown.

'I'll be ready. Don't worry.' Max sat up, rubbing her sore head.

Her mother's eyes then landed on Linden's hair, which stared back at her like a hedgehog after a bad fright.

'You are going to do something with that . . . aren't you?' she said with an obvious streak of horror in her voice.

But before Linden could answer, she spun from the room. 'We'll never make it!' she wailed, her voice fading, until she suddenly spring-loaded herself back into the room and onto Max's bed. She held her daughter's face in her hands.

'I love you, sweetie, you know that, don't you?' She blinked away some sudden tears and hugged Max firmly before leaping from the bed and continuing on her cyclonic way.

'When should I tell her I *have* done my hair?' Linden stood in front of the mirror and tried to make a few minor adjustments to his wild hair. 'I spent a good ten minutes on this do.' He turned back to Max. 'Everything's normal around here, then?'

'Yep.' Max sighed. 'Normal as it gets. One minute she's relaxed and happy, the next she's acting like she's been let loose from the jaws of hell.'

'Makes for an interesting life.'

'If by interesting you mean everything sane has been kidnapped.'

Kidnapped . . . Max's face fell as she remembered her dream. When she'd called Toby's house the day she saw him in the park, his aunt told her he was staying late at school. Max knew that wasn't true but had no choice other than to thank her and hang up. 'Linden, what would your mum say is happening when you dream about someone?'

He offered her a fake look of embarrassment. 'Max, are you dreaming about me, again? I guess it's not your fault, I am a good-looking man.'

Max gave Linden a pained smile. 'Your mum must have had a theory on it.'

'She said it meant you had something to sort out with that person. Why?'

'Nothing.' She tried to shake the thought of Toby out of her head. Today was going to be hard enough without him on her mind. 'There's no getting out of this wedding, is there?'

'Not unless your mum suddenly comes down with amnesia and forgets who you are.' Linden stood up to leave. 'Just remember, we've survived plane crashes, death chambers, and rooms of jelly and worms, so we can survive your mother's wedding.'

He gave her a grin that was a Linden special. 'See you downstairs, chief.'

'OK,' she said, before adding, 'You look good, by the way.'

Linden ran his hand through his billowing hair. 'It's my natural beauty.'

'And I thought it was the suit,' Max offered.

'That's only part of it.' He sighed grandly and left.

Max smiled. It was as if Linden had this zone of calm all around him—and she knew she needed as much calm as she could get if she was going to make it to the end of the day.

Especially wearing a dress.

She opened her wardrobe door. There it was. Hanging innocently. Staring at her as if what she was about to do was no big deal. It wasn't that Max didn't like the dress, it was more that she and dresses in general didn't get along. Her mother had even let her choose it. It was red with a deep crimson pattern of Japanese script embroidered along the neck and hem. Simple, discreet, and hopefully would attract very little attention.

Max steeled herself. People wear them every day, she thought. How hard could it be?

At that moment, the three stylists her mother had booked came streaming through her door carrying bags, brushes, and hairdryers, as if they were shoppers from an end-of-year sale. For the next hour, Max felt as though she'd been pulled into the arms of a hyperactive octopus. She was prodded, brushed, sprayed, and covered in face creams, powders, and make-up, before being tugged into her dress. The three stylists then proudly held up a mirror.

'What do you think?'

Max looked down at the floor. 'Good. Fine. Thanks,' she mumbled.

She knew no matter how hard they tried, they weren't going to create a princess out of what they had to work with. And just as quickly as they'd swirled into the room, they gathered their things and left.

Max sighed and raised her head towards the mirror, dreading what she would see. First she saw her red sandals, then the dress. She raised her head a little further and finally she saw her hair, which had been curled just a little.

She stood straighter, happy that what she saw wasn't a total disaster. 'Linden's right. We have dealt with much scarier things than this.'

She took her Spy Force medallion from a hidden compartment in her chest of drawers and tucked it into her dress so it was completely concealed. She then cautiously opened her bedroom door. Down the landing, her mother's room was spilling over with people and noise. Max watched as designers, hairdressers, and men arranging flowered bouquets fussed and fawned. She walked away quickly before she could get sucked inside, and made her way downstairs.

Outside the lounge room door, she heard the sound of Ben's and Eleanor's laughter. It was the sanest noise she'd heard all morning and she rushed in to join them, but when she opened the door, the laughter was replaced by a shocked silence and the three dazed faces of Ben, Eleanor, and Linden.

Max's bravado fell from her like a collapsing building. 'It's bad, isn't it?'

No one said anything. They just kept staring.

The dress that felt fine before now sat on Max's skin as if it was made of prickles.

'Someone needs to say something. Quickly,' she cautioned.

Eleanor scooped her up among her layers of white linen skirts and shawls. 'Max, you look so . . . beautiful.'

Ben wore a goofy smile. 'Every man there won't be able to stop looking at you. Lucky I'll be there to fend them off.'

But there was one person who hadn't said anything.

Linden. He looked as if he'd been slapped in the face with a wet fish.

'Doesn't she look like a pearl, Linden?' Ben asked pointedly.

Still Linden just stood there. He opened his mouth and tried to say something, but nothing came out. Ben slapped him on the back as if he'd stopped breathing, and finally Linden said, 'You look amazing.'

Max just managed to hold back a huge smile. 'Thanks, but you don't have to say that.'

'I know.'

Linden kept staring. Ben and Eleanor exchanged a cheeky smile.

'Max!' Max's mother's footsteps bounded down the stairs. 'Are you ready yet?' She barged into the lounge room with a large white smock over her dress. Half her hair was curled and dotted with flowers, while the other half was still in heat curlers.

Max turned and straightened out her dress, hoping her mother would like how she looked.

'Oh, hello, everyone. Good, you're ready. Help yourselves to anything in the kitchen. Can't stay. The cars are almost here.'

She turned and disappeared.

Ben turned to Linden. 'You in?'

For once, the mention of food didn't catch Linden's attention.

'Linden?' Ben asked as Linden's staring at Max went on. 'Food?'

'Oh yeah. Right,' he mumbled and followed Ben out.

Max watched the space where her mother had just been standing and sank into the sofa, feeling small and invisible. 'She didn't say anything.'

Eleanor sat beside Max and took her hand. 'You really do look lovely.'

There were times when Max guiltily wished it was Eleanor who was her mum. 'I don't mean to sound horrible, but are you sure you two are sisters?'

Eleanor stroked her niece's cheek. 'She's just distracted. It's a big day.'

'I bet you weren't like this when you got married.'

Eleanor smiled and stayed silent. Max knew this meant she wasn't.

'What was your wedding like?'

'Ben and I got married in bare feet on a beach down the coast. We giggled so much we had sore cheeks for three days.'

Max could see it all. No fuss, no stylists, and no expensive dresses, just Eleanor and Ben looking like they always did, except maybe Ben would be dressed better.

Then it struck her. 'How come you never had kids?'

'We wanted to but we couldn't.' A brief flicker of sadness rippled across Eleanor's face. 'Besides, we've got you.'

Sometimes Eleanor said things that made Max want to cry, and this was one of those times. Max flung herself into the white, cottony layers of Eleanor's shawl, just as Ben and Linden came out of the kitchen carrying giant sandwiches that only just fitted on their plates.

'That is one well-packed fridge. Linden and I think we might move in for a while if that's OK.'

Linden sat on the sofa, looking awkward, and bit into his sandwich.

The doorbell chimed from the hall and a

panicked call sounded from upstairs. 'The cars are here!'

A tangle of fuss and high-pitched shrieking erupted as Max's mother and her followers exploded into the hall. They stopped in front of a hanging mirror as hairdressers finished shaping curls, manicurists put the final buff to nails, and make-up artists applied the last strokes of lip gloss and waterproof mascara.

Squeals of laughter followed as they then hurried out of the door of the apartment. Eleanor saw Max deflate as her mother passed her without a word. She held her face in her hands and gave her one of her duvet-warm smiles.

'Let's you, Ben, Linden, and I have a fabulous day. Deal?'

'I'll be in that,' Ben chirped in. 'Especially as I am going to be with the two most beautiful women in the whole place.' His last word got caught in his throat and Max knew that was a definite sign he was going to cry.

'It's true,' Linden let out in a strange voice that sounded very un-Linden-like.

Oh no, thought Max, they're both going to cry.

An awkward pause bloated around them like

an overfed goldfish. Max was keen to avoid any tears and any more of Linden's staring, which was starting to freak her out. 'We'd better get going.'

'You're right.' Ben wiped away a tear and followed Max as they hurried down the stairs to the front of the building.

As Max reached the door to the street, she felt relieved that at least for the rest of the day, all the attention would be on her mother. But as she opened the door of the building, she held her hands up to shield her eyes from the lights of what seemed like a million flashing cameras. Every newspaper and magazine had turned up on their front doorstep to get a glimpse of the happy bride. Or, more likely, didn't just turn up but were actually invited. Max had thought it was her mother's wedding but suddenly, in the turning of a door handle, it had become the rest of the world's.

Max blinked into the blinding white light. She put her foot out to find the next step but missed and was sent free-falling through the swarm of camera operators piled onto the stairs.

'Max!' Ben pushed his way through to catch her as she toppled downwards.

None of the photographers moved to help as Max somersaulted through the air and stumbled over every step until she landed with an ungracious and final thud at the bottom.

'Max?'

Ben's throat tightened as he shoved the camera clickers out of the way. Max lay at the bottom of the stairs, her arms awry and her legs bent at a horrible angle.

CHAPTER 6
AN UNINVITED GUEST

After Max had come to a stop and figured out how to make her hands pull her dress down to cover her brand new undies, she felt someone lift her from the ground.

'Are you all right, sunshine? Tell me what you feel. Have you broken any bones? Can you breathe OK? Where does it hurt?'

Max wasn't sure where to start. 'Everywhere, I think. What happened?'

'You had a bit of a fall.'

The fall. She remembered the blur of white flashes she had fallen past as she tumbled towards the car, and thought how they'd all make a perfect front cover picture for any one of the magazines and newspapers that were there.

Linden and Eleanor finally managed to push their way through the media pack as Ben helped Max to her feet. 'Is that OK? Do you feel woozy? Do you know who you are?'

'I know I'm a total klutz and that I have to get out of here before I do anything else to embarrass myself.'

'Good.' Linden smiled in relief. 'She's fine.'

Ben helped Max into the main car, where she nestled gingerly beside her mother, who hadn't seen a thing.

'Sweetie, there you are,' she said as if she was seeing Max for the first time that day. 'Sorry about the cameras. I knew there'd be *some* media but I never thought there'd be as much as this.'

Max shifted slightly on her seat, her left bottom cheek hurting from where she had fallen. 'Will this be on the news tonight?'

'Probably.' Her mother said it as if it was almost as important as the getting married part. 'Isn't that great? All your friends at school will see you.'

Suddenly the pain of sitting down was minuscule compared to the one eating into her pride. Great, she thought, as if the kids at school don't have enough reasons to make fun of me. Max was stuck in the gloom of future embarrassment when she noticed her mother smiling at her. Not a regular smile, but one she hadn't seen for ages.

'You look so very beautiful, Max.'

Max stared, making sure her mother meant her. She'd never used the words 'Max' and 'beautiful' in the same sentence before.

'Thank you for being part of this.' She pulled Max into her dress for a warm hug. 'I love you so much it makes me want to cry.'

Max winced as her mother hugged her sore arms. She'd wanted her mum to notice her, but now that she had, it felt strange. Then Max remembered another time someone had hugged her after she was hurt. It was on the ski fields in Aspen and that time it was her dad.*

Max blinked away the tears that now blurred her vision. The thought of her dad could do that. Her mother rarely hugged her, and never like she was now. For a moment Max felt as if she was a kid again and her mum and dad were still together and she never had to go too far before one of them would lift her into a hug that was like sleeping in clouds.

The car pulled up at the church, where an equally large squadron of cameras was waiting for them. Max looked up at her mother, but she looked so happy Max couldn't bring herself to complain. Instead she said something else.

'I'm really happy for you, Mum.'

Her mother leant in and kissed her on the cheek. 'Thank you.'

Ben opened the door. 'Your escort is ready.'

Max's grandfather had died when she was young so Ben had volunteered to walk her mother down the aisle.

* See *Max Remy Spy Force: The Hollywood Mission*

Max's mum stepped out of the car and onto the red carpet that led to the entrance of the church. She smiled elegantly and waved into the glare of the lights as if she'd just arrived at the Academy Awards. Max, on the other hand, fumbled out behind her and looked as if she was being attacked by a swarm of bees.

'You're first, sweetie.'

Her mother had organized that Max would lead the wedding party as a treat but she might as well have thrown her into a pit of crawling cockroaches for all the joy she was going to get out of it.

Max started a silent chant in her head. 'Please don't fall down. Please don't fall down.'

Linden and Eleanor were standing nearby and Max caught the same cow-staring look on Linden's face as before. He smiled, but not with his usual grin—more of a soppy, sad-movie kind of grin.

The music started and Eleanor blew her a kiss before she nudged a dazed Linden into the church. Max breathed deeply and turned to Ben, who gave her a wink, ready to follow her lead as he stood beside her mum.

Max walked through the flashing lights, up a small set of stairs and into the beginnings of her mother's wedding.

Inside, twisting stems of red bougainvillea were draped on the ends of the wooden pews, which were packed with people Max didn't know, smiling at her lovingly as if they'd known her from childhood. There was a second level of seating above, which was reserved for more cameras and journalists hurriedly taking notes.

At the end of the aisle was a glass-domed roof that sent shafts of frosted light onto a huge marble altar. And before the altar was Aidan. He wore a light-blue suit and no tie, trying for ultra-casual, but Max knew that he'd probably spent days getting ready and that the suit had cost the same as a small island. He gave her one of those toothpaste grins he'd obviously practised in the mirror.

Then she remembered. In a short while that same grinning man would be her stepfather. The thought instantly tripped her up and sent her staggering towards one of the seats. A woman wearing a hat that looked like a white fluffy cat caught her and smiled through a thick, wrinkled layer of make-up. Max righted herself and mumbled a quiet thank you.

Finally she reached the altar and, as rehearsed, stepped aside to make room for Ben and her mum. Ben kissed her mother on the cheek before moving next to Max. Her mother then stepped up to Aidan and the two held hands and grinned like kids who've had too much sugar.

The minister soon got to the part of the ceremony where he asked if anyone knew any reason why the marriage shouldn't go ahead. Max looked around. Maybe now someone would stop it. Maybe her dad would burst into the church in his usual floppy clothes and demand the wedding be stopped, pleading with her mother not to marry Aidan and declaring that it was he who really loved her. Max knew it was all very soap, but it didn't stop her from wishing it was real.

No one said anything and neither Max's dad nor his floppy clothes appeared.

The minister continued, raising his voice a little as they heard the sound of an approaching chopper.

Excellent, Max thought, now we've got TV cameras above us as well.

The chopper seemed to be approaching swiftly, its swooping blades becoming louder. The minister tried to ignore it, until he couldn't be heard over the whirring noise.

Max's mother looked around, smiling nervously.

A shadow appeared above the glass-domed

roof, cutting off the falling streams of light. Three large discs attached themselves to the glass with a suctioning thud. Small screams and quiet gasps filled the echoing church interior.

Max was looking at Ben, wanting him to explain what was happening, when a large glass-cutter jabbed into the dome and began slicing out a rounded hole.

Shouts of panic splintered through the church. The minister tried in vain to keep everyone calm as guests began climbing over seats, scrambling down balconies and pushing their way to the exits.

'Mum!' Max saw her mother's frightened face but she couldn't be heard over the piercing noise.

Ben took Max's hand and looked down the aisle to see a bulge of terrified, jostling people. He scanned the chaos until he caught Eleanor's eye, signalling for her and Linden to get out. He then moved to protect Max's mother but, before he could reach her, the cutter finished its job. A huge circular slab of glass was wrenched from the dome and great clouds of smoke billowed through the hole, filling the church with thick fog.

'Mum!' Max desperately reached into the fog, trying to grasp her mother's hand. Through the mist, she could see a figure moving on the altar, carrying something large. They then moved upwards, as if they were being hoisted towards the roof.

The noise of the chopper swirled away.

'Ben?' Max asked, unsure what had happened as an anxious silence settled inside the church.

'I'm here, sweetheart.' He held her hand firmly and led her towards the altar. They were waving away the smoke, feeling their way through, when Max felt something against her foot.

'Mum?' She knelt down and saw Aidan through the clearing mist, a bleeding gash in his forehead.

Ben knelt down and felt for his pulse.

'He's OK. He's taken a nasty hit, though.' He took out a hanky and laid it against Aidan's head.

'Ben, where's Mum?' Max asked. Ben was someone who could make things right, who could give her an answer that meant she could stop panicking. But when they searched the rest of the church they knew their worst fears were real.

Max's mum had been kidnapped.

CHAPTER 7
A SPY FORCE PLAN AND A SURPRISING VISITOR

'How does that feel?'

Eleanor had helped Max into her pyjamas and tucked a blanket around her on the sofa before placing a cold pack on her forehead.

'It's OK.'

Max didn't know what she felt. Ever since she'd left the church she'd had this weird feeling of walking through clear gel. Everything looked normal on one level, but on another, it was all completely strange.

Her emotions swung up and down like a seesaw. One minute she wanted to jump up, break through the gel and make everything normal again. The next, she felt as if all her energy had been sucked out of her, leaving her lying uselessly on the sofa like a rag doll.

'Can I get you anything else?'

Max looked into the kind eyes of her aunt. 'No. Thanks, Eleanor. I . . . I . . .' Max gripped her hands together beneath the blanket. 'I know I was bad at showing it, but I really love my mum.'

'I know, honey. And she knows that too.'

'Does she?' Tears straggled their way down Max's face. 'But I never told her.'

Eleanor held her close. 'Believe me, Max, she

knew it. Sometimes you don't have to say things out loud for people to know it.'

Linden came out of the kitchen carrying a mug. 'I've brought you a hot chocolate. Mum used to say hot drinks make everything feel better. I shaved some real chocolate on the top. I don't do that for many people. So you should consider yourself very special.'

Max smiled for the first time since leaving the church. 'Thanks, Linden.'

'No problem. They're pretty easy to make.'

'No, I mean for the jokes . . . for you.' She stopped trying to explain. 'You know what I mean.'

Linden smiled awkwardly. 'Well, the jokes *are* good, but the chocolate is too.' He placed the mug on the table beside Max. 'I'll leave it here.'

In the silence that followed, Max slowly scanned the room. It was strewn with ribboned boxes, presents, bunches of flowers, and cards that spilled onto almost every surface. They sat as a constant reminder of what had happened. And the one thought she couldn't block out.

She was a spy, she'd completed all sorts of missions, but the time when she was needed most, she didn't do a thing.

Ben leaned into the curtains, staring vacantly

at the sky outside. He'd been there ever since they returned home. Max knew by the slump of his shoulders and the way he hadn't said anything that he was thinking the same thing about himself.

'Uncle Ben?'

He kept staring out of the window. 'We'll find your mum, Max. I promise.' His words were full of guilt and sadness.

The door then opened behind them.

'Hope you don't mind that we let ourselves in.'

Max saw Steinberger holding a silent lock-opening device, standing beside a serious-faced Harrison.

'Thank you for coming so soon.' Eleanor welcomed them in.

'The Invisible Jet still does a great job,' Steinberger said.

Harrison walked over to Max. 'How are you dropping down?' He winced, aware that this wasn't a good time to mix up his words. 'I mean . . . *holding up?*'

'I'm all right. I . . .' Max had to pause to stop herself from crying.

Harrison looked around the room. 'Is everyone else OK?'

'We're fine,' Eleanor answered. 'How is Aidan?'

'He's in hospital for observation,' Steinberger answered. 'It seems he was knocked out pretty soundly and doesn't remember much more than what you told us on the palm computer. We'll question him further after he's rested.'

Max looked up at Harrison and spoke in a small, frightened voice. 'I want to find my mum.'

'We will, Max. There are agents on the job right now working on just that.'

Steinberger took out his palm computer and entered in several codes. 'Fortunately there were plenty of TV crews and cameras at the church to capture everything that happened. Our agents are equipped with ultra-powerful magnifying glasses and digital tape machines capable of analysing every frame of a photo or video image. They also have an X-ray component that can see through the objects in the picture as well.' He looked reassuringly at Max. 'Whoever did this won't be able to hide a thing.'

'So you can find out who did it?' Linden asked.

'We'll be able to get a complete fix on their faces, and with our International Computer Identity system, we should have the results in a few hours.'

'Do you think it's Blue?' Max felt a surge of panic shoot through her like an electrical charge.

Ben turned his head slightly towards Harrison, while the others sat rigid with anticipation, waiting for what their chief had to say.

'Blacksea Penitentiary is one of the most secure prisons in world. Every piece of information that enters or leaves is intercepted and analysed. We're in direct contact with the guards and only minutes ago they assured me that Blue is in his cell.'

'Do they know he's really there and not just a projection?' Max thought back to Blue's use of the Spectral Hologram Mark III during their mission to save the Annual Spy Awards Night.* What she had thought was him was merely his projected image.

'He's there,' Steinberger confirmed. 'The guards conduct random and routine physical checks. And . . .' He frowned. 'By all accounts, he's a model prisoner.'

'Well, that proves it,' Linden said wryly. 'It can't be him.'

He smiled at Max, wanting desperately for her

* See *Max Remy Spy Force: The Nightmare Vortex*

to feel better, but realized none of his regular jokes would do it this time.

'So it wasn't Blue?' Eleanor tried to conceal her fear for her sister's life.

'It would be almost impossible to organize from where he is.' It was obvious from the look on Harrison's face that this wasn't the first time he'd thought about this question. 'However, the more impossible the task, the more determined Blue is to make it happen.'

Max gulped in a clutch of air as another rush of dread sank into her. 'But why Mum? Why not take me or Ben? We were there too!' She stopped, her breaths short and sharp, realizing what she had said. She turned towards her uncle. 'I don't mean I'd want them to take you, Ben. I'd never want that. It's just that . . .'

'I know what you mean,' Ben answered softly.

He caught Max's eye, desperately wanting her to know it was OK, but they also both knew that this might be Blue's way of unleashing his cruellest revenge on them yet.

'We have to do something!' Max again felt a wave of panic.

Harrison fixed her with a solemn eye. 'After our initial investigations are complete, we will have a more solid picture of who is behind this and why, but until then you will all stay put.'

Max knew Harrison was serious, but she wanted so badly to save her mum that her skin felt as if it was crawling with ants.

It was then the doorbell rang.

Max went to leap up but Harrison's warning voice made her stop. 'Max!'

'I'll get it,' Linden offered.

'Whoever it is, tell them we'll call them at a better time,' Eleanor advised.

Linden nodded and went to the door, where he was surprised to find Toby. He was the one person who topped the list of people who weren't welcome in Max's life.

'Toby. Hi.'

'Linden!' Toby grinned wildly. Then frowned. The two had met when Linden visited Max for a week and came with her to school. Toby hadn't thought much of Linden then, but now he was standing in front of him, he wanted to plug him in the shoulder and arm-wrestle him as if they were best friends.

Then the weirdest thing happened. His head filled with strange images, all of them with Max and Linden. They were in a fancy restaurant, in a movie studio, and in a dungeon where Linden lay at the bottom of a deep pit.*

Toby had no idea where these images came from, but somehow he felt as if they'd really happened. 'Is Max in?'

Toby went to walk past but Linden put out his arm and stopped him.

'Now isn't great. I'll ask Max to call you later.'

'But I'm here now. I'll only be a minute.'

Toby ducked under Linden's arm and headed towards the lounge, where he could hear voices. 'Sounds like there's a party going on.'

Linden followed him as he flung the door open and stared at the people gathered around Max. Toby didn't know who they were but he had the strangest feeling he'd met them all before. 'Hi, my name's Toby. Max and I go to the same school. Don't we, Max?'

'I tried to keep him out but he got past me,' Linden explained.

'It's OK,' Eleanor said gently as Max sank back into the sofa.

There was an awkward silence. Toby noticed Max's pale and drawn face.

* See *Max Remy Spy Force: The Hollywood Mission*

'Aunt Mabel said you called.' He felt suddenly uncertain. 'I left messages, but when you didn't call back I thought I'd come over.'

Max pulled the blanket higher over her pyjamas. The day had been one of the worst in her life, and Toby seeing her in this state was only making it worse. 'Don't bother saying anything about how awful I look. Whatever you're thinking, I already know I look worse.'

Toby said nothing. He knew from Max's voice that something terrible had happened. He also knew he probably should leave, but his feet wouldn't move.

Eleanor stood up and walked towards him. 'It's been a bit of a rough day, Toby. Maybe Max could call you when she's feeling better.'

'Sure.' Toby wanted to stay and make sure Max was OK, to ask what was wrong and see if he could help, but he also had to tell her something.

'Mum and Dad have to stay in Europe for the rest of the year and they want me to go and live with them,' he blurted out as Eleanor opened the door for him.

Linden saw an even deeper sadness settle in Max's eyes.

'When?' Max asked softly.

'In two weeks.' Toby paused. 'I just wanted to tell you.'

Max was silent. Now she knew why Toby had looked so sad in the park. His parents were heart specialists who'd been working in Austria for the last few months. He'd stayed at home so he wouldn't interrupt school, but also because he didn't want to leave his friends. Now it looked as if he was going to have to leave them for good.

'Do you have to go?' Max felt the ache in her chest suddenly get worse.

'Mum and Dad have already organized it.'

Toby paused. He and Max had never been friends, but when he'd found out about his parents' plan, Max was the first person he wanted to tell.

'Well, I'll see you later then.' Toby walked out of the room and, seconds later, the front door clicked shut after him.

Eleanor settled herself even closer to Max and kissed her on the forehead. Harrison nodded to Steinberger, who handed him a tape.

'Here's a copy of all the video taken at the wedding. I know it may be difficult to look at, but it might give you more of an idea as to what happened,' Harrison said. 'We will be in touch as soon as we know more and have a further plan of action.'

Max carefully took the tape.

'Agents Canon and Crampton are positioned downstairs,' Steinberger explained. 'You can contact them with your palm computers if you need anything. They will also be watching the area for any suspicious behaviour, so you are completely safe.'

Linden flinched. He hadn't thought they might be in danger as well.

'The news will also be on every network and front page throughout the country, so the media attention is going to be fierce. The agents will also be in charge of keeping them away.'

Max said nothing as she stared at the tape.

'Eleanor, I'll leave it to you to call Linden's dad. Max, your principal knows what has happened and understands that you'll be away from school for a few days.' He smiled gently. 'By then everything should be back to normal.'

Harrison walked over to Max and wiped her fringe out of her eyes. 'Your mother will be fine, Max. With all the agents and resources we have on the case, she will be back home with you very soon.'

Max saw in Harrison's eyes that he would do everything he could to make this happen. She wanted to believe him, wanted everything he said to be true, but as her head ached and her chest felt locked in a twisting vice, what she wanted more was for this day to have never happened.

CHAPTER 8
A STARTLING DEATH

The lounge room filled with a blue flickering glow as the video played again. Always the same beginning and, no matter how many times Max watched, always the same end. The wedding, the laughter, the smiles, followed by the helicopter, the thick wall of smoke and her mother's disappearance.

She scanned the screen for any clue that would tell her who did it. The sight of a face, the calling out of a name. There had to be something, anything that would help her find her mum.

Max came to the part where her mother joined Aidan at the altar. She looked so happy and confident. As if she was untouchable. That was the thing about her mother. She was so brave and outspoken that Max had thought those things would always keep her safe. Even after her parents' divorce when her mother was so sad, she still looked strong. It never seemed possible that anything bad could ever happen to her.

Max heard the first sounds of the helicopter as it approached the church, followed soon after by the chaos of screaming and scrambling guests. Finally the image tilted as the camera was dropped and, lying face up, recorded the glass-cutter doing its job. Feet jumped over the camera and knocked into it as the plumes of smoke filled the room, until one sharp kick sent the image black.

Again the same ending, and again her mother had disappeared.

Max flinched as a gentle knock landed on the lounge room door.

Ben entered carrying a tray with cheese on toast, two cups and a pot of tea.

Max wiped her pyjama sleeves against her reddened eyes and tried to smile but it came out more as a grimace.

'Whenever things go wrong at the farm, Eleanor and I have this rule that we sit down and have a cup of tea and cheese on toast before we do anything. Not sure what it is, but afterwards even the really bad stuff feels better. Just between you and me, I think it's the sitting with Eleanor that does it.'

Ben hadn't been able to talk to Max all afternoon and she knew his effort to be cheerful now was all for her.

'Thanks, but I don't think I can eat anything.'

Ben looked down at the toast and steaming tea. 'You know what? Neither can I.' He pushed the tray across the coffee table. 'Maybe we'll just do the sitting part.'

Neither of them knew what to say next, but after seconds had passed in silence, Max couldn't stand it. 'When are we going to hear from Steinberger and Harrison? It's been ages and we haven't heard anything.'

'They'll contact us as soon as they can.' Ben smiled. 'They're Spy Force, remember? They're the best.'

'But what if something's happening to her? What if she's being hurt? What if . . .'

Max stopped, afraid of what the real answers might be. She'd been finding it hard to stop her brain from imagining all sorts of terrible situations for her mother.

'Max,' Ben said sadly, his hands squeezed in front of him, 'I'm so sorry about today. I've been going over and over what happened and I should have saved your mum. I was standing right there and I . . .'

Ben pressed his lips together tightly. Max had never seen him so sad.

'It's all my fault, Max.' His words were like sharp spikes digging into him.

'Uncle Ben.' Max stared into his eyes. 'That's not true.'

'But I should have—'

Max interrupted. 'I've watched this video again and again and as much as I don't want to admit it, you and I couldn't have done anything. Not with the way it happened. But the thing is, it doesn't make me feel any better. I just want her back.'

Ben's strong arms pulled Max into a warm hug. 'Me too.'

Max held on to her uncle as if she was falling and holding on to him was the only thing stopping her from crashing to the ground.

Linden and Eleanor poked their heads in from the hallway.

'Can we come in?'

'Yes,' Max snuffled. 'I'd like that.'

Linden noticed the tray. 'Don't blame you for not wanting that. When it comes to cheese on toast, Ben needs a few lessons.'

'I didn't know it was such an art.' Ben raised his eyebrows.

'Oh, it is,' Linden replied importantly. 'And only a few of us ever really master it.'

Ben slugged Linden with a pillow and Max smiled as it landed on his head. Linden was about to retaliate when they heard a small beeping noise come from Eleanor's pocket. She pulled out her palm computer and switched it on.

'It's Steinberger.'

The now-familiar feeling of panic barged its way into Max's chest.

'Hello, all. How are you?' Steinberger's face appeared on a direct link from Spy Force HQ in London.

'Better,' Eleanor replied for them. 'We're eager to hear what you've learnt.'

'Yes, of course you are. We are very close to discovering the identities of the kidnappers, but I'm afraid until we have conclusive proof we can't say any more.' He saw Max's face fall. 'Sorry, Max, but we do have something else.'

Steinberger's face was replaced by the image of a newsreader. She sat beside a background picture of Mr Blue with a caption beneath that said, 'Tragic Death'.

Eleanor turned up the volume as the others huddled around the computer.

'. . . Prison wardens say they aren't sure how the fire started, but a full investigation into the tragedy will be launched immediately. This report from Jack Keenan.'

A suited and windswept journalist appeared on the screen. 'This is Blacksea Penitentiary, where a little after noon today a fire broke out in the cafeteria as the prisoners were sitting down to lunch. Wardens immediately began fire drill procedures, rounding up the men and quickly escorting them to assembly areas. But it was the heroism of one man that attracted the attention of the guards.'

A prison guard with his shirt and tie undone and his face and hair wiped through with soot spoke next.

'It has to be the bravest thing I've ever seen. He kept going back into the burning building and carrying men out over his shoulders.' The guard wiped his eyes. 'The last time he went in, he never came out. I'll never forget it as long as I live.'

Linden watched the screen, as mystified as the others about Blue's supposed heroics. 'What's going on? Blue wouldn't save his own grandmother from a fire.'

The reporter then went on to describe Blue's achievements and successes. Ben sniffed at the mention of Blue's great work at the Department of Science and New Technologies.

Max listened to the tributes and awards as well as praise for his work with charities and animal conservation.

'I guess they're not going to mention the bit about why he was in prison,' Linden scoffed.

The report finished with mourners placing flowers outside a white, nondescript Georgian house in London, supposedly Blue's home, which was fringed with brightly coloured window boxes and had the appearance that no megalomaniac had ever lived there.

Linden spoke up as Steinberger reappeared on the screen. 'Is he really dead?'

'It does appear so.' He seemed as perplexed as they were.

'I'm not sure about you, Steinby, but there's something about this brave death I don't buy,' Ben snarled.

'We've been in contact with the Blacksea wardens, who have told us the fire happened exactly as the news reported. They've confirmed that Blue died and his body is lying in their morgue.'

Ben, Eleanor, Max, and Linden all knew what they'd seen and heard but they also knew that when it came to how Blue operated, what you saw was rarely what you got, and they weren't quite ready to believe the story just yet.

Max slowly pulled the blanket higher under

her chin and sank lower into the soft cushions of the sofa. As the news of Blue's death circled in her head, she could think of only one thing.

'If Blue is dead, who kidnapped my mother?'

CHAPTER 9

A CLOSE CALL, A BOMB BLAST, AND A SHATTERED NIGHT

As the burnt orange light of sunset faded and the street lights flickered into life, Quimby turned her small red hatchback into her quiet leafy street and sighed. It had been a long day. She loved her work as Spy Force inventor but this was the part of the day she loved most. Driving home and seeing Millie, her cat, parading along the windowsill as if she was a model on a Paris catwalk.

'You scamp,' Quimby whispered affectionately as she pulled up in front of her house.

She walked up the stairs and tapped on the window beside the door. 'Hello there. Doing a bit of styling for me then?'

Millie mewed and rubbed her body into the white curtains so her fur became a ruffled mess.

Quimby pushed her dark, tumbling hair out of her eyes, trying to tuck it under her bright red scarf with one hand, while fumbling through her bag for her keys with the other. 'I've got a surprise for you,' she said excitedly to Millie. 'One that's going to make you love me even more.'

She found her keys beneath a muddle of papers, mints, Plantorium lip balm and various wires, diodes, and transistors, but as she put her key in the door, a bullet splintered into the wooden frame near her hand.

Millie leapt from the windowsill out of view as Quimby stopped still, the smell of burning wood and hot metal itching her nose. She gulped short sharp breaths as her hand sat frozen on the key. She tried to make it move so she could get inside as another shot was fired and whistled towards her. Quimby ducked as a bullet drove a hole all the way through her front door.

This time her hand worked quickly. Turning the key, she opened the door and slipped into the hallway, crouching down just before another bullet shot past and lodged firmly in the wood of her fourth stair.

Keeping low, Quimby kicked the door shut and crawled into the sitting room to beneath the window. She rose slowly upwards, hiding behind the curtain, inching her way into a position where she could just see the street.

It was then she saw him. A man in black leather sitting on a motorbike. He was staring straight at her. He revved the bike twice before it screamed into life and tore down the street in a black blur.

Quimby slid back to the floor, her heart beating so hard it hurt. She flinched when she felt Millie's fur against her limp hand.

'Millie, darling,' she breathed in relief.

She lifted the frightened cat into her arms. Millie mewed again and snuggled into Quimby's embrace.

'It's OK,' she said in a quivering whisper as she stroked Millie's head. 'It's over now.'

Professor Plomb, the Spy Force explosions expert who had a terrible fear of loud noises, adjusted his ear muffs and walked into the supermarket carpark, weaving carefully through the aisles of cars. Two kids behind him pointed and laughed at his unusual ear-wear, but he didn't hear any of it.

As he approached his car, he deactivated the alarm with a wheep-wheep he also didn't hear. Fumbling with his keys, he dropped them into a small puddle.

'Oh, blast.'

He picked them up and shook them out, before spotting his car parked a few spaces away. He smiled. He was almost there. But as he started walking towards it, the car exploded into a fiery ball, sending pieces of metal, leather, and plastic high into the air.

Plomb dropped to the ground, clutching his bag of shopping. Screaming parents covered their children and scuttled them back towards the supermarket or into cars before driving quickly away. Security guards seemed to emerge from nowhere to direct shoppers away from the explosion site, speaking hurriedly into their two-way radios as hundreds of car alarms went off at once.

Plomb lay where he was, moving each limb slightly to check he was OK. He looked up to see his wrecked car scattered throughout the carpark in broken, melting pieces, on bonnets and roofs of cars and on the blackened asphalt all around him.

Apart from a bump to the forehead and a painful elbow which had taken the brunt of his fall, he was OK. Plomb quietly stood up, tucked his squashed shopping beneath his arm, and hurriedly walked away from the scene of the explosive attack.

Steinberger climbed the stairs to the entrance of his apartment building. He stopped in front of the double layer of letterboxes and, taking out a small gold key, opened the padlock and collected his mail. There were flyers for plumbing and carpet cleaning companies and several bills, but one letter looked interesting. It was addressed to R. L. Steinberger, Esquire. He liked that. 'Esquire'. It made him sound important, perhaps even a little noble. It was an embossed envelope with a sweeping royal-blue script.

He tucked the envelopes and flyers under his arm and climbed the rest of the stairs to his humble sixth-floor apartment. The twinkling lights of the evening filled his bay window and, after switching on the light and tossing the mail on a sideboard, he walked over to his two potted plants by the window.

'Hello, my lovelies.'

He leant down and, like every other night, read the tag attached to one of the pots.

Some of the Plantorium's finest especially for you,
Love Frond

Steinberger's pulse quickened and he sighed happily, before moving to the kitchen to put the kettle on for a cup of tea.

He then grabbed his mail and sank into his sofa beside the plants. He opened the few bills and skimmed the flyers, leaving the embossed letter until last. When he opened it, he found a disk and a letter with one simple line:

Look out of your window

Steinberger winced through a half-smile, trying to guess the meaning of the few words.

Kneeling on the sofa and craning his head out of the window in puzzlement, he saw a man in a motorcycle helmet and black leather outfit standing beneath a street lamp. The man lifted a gun as if in slow motion. Steinberger frowned, trying to understand what was happening.

And then he did.

He dived into the sofa just as a piercing blast exploded above him, followed by a spray of glass and splinters of wood. He pulled a cushion over his head and jammed his face into the soft seat. The sound of shattering glass seemed to last whole minutes, as outside he heard the growling of a motorbike.

Steinberger carefully rolled off the sofa, scuttled to a different window and peeked out from behind the frame.

It was as if the man on the bike was waiting for

just this moment. He gave one last roaring rev of his engine before slamming shut his helmet's visor and letting the bike loose in a screeching exit down the street.

Steinberger flinched as he blinked away a trickle of blood from his gashed forehead. He took a hanky from his jacket pocket and dabbed at his bloodied brow. It was numb, but from the amount of blood absorbed by the hanky, he'd need stitches.

He stared around his dust- and glass-sprayed room that had moments earlier been filled with the quiet of a late London evening. He stood in confusion, not knowing what to do or think, trying to work out who had done this and why.

Then his mind stilled and his heart fell at what he saw next.

The fallen potted palms that lay spilled and uprooted at his feet.

CHAPTER 10
A CLEVER DISGUISE AND AN ALARMING DECISION

'A professional killer has been hired to kill, or at least scare, Spy Force agents.'

Max and Linden gaped, wide-eyed, at what they'd been told. Ben slipped his hand into Eleanor's, squeezing it protectively.

They'd been summoned by Harrison to his office at Spy Force Headquarters in London and, using the Time and Space Machine, they had managed to get there in a matter of minutes. They now sat on two leather sofas facing Harrison's large oak desk. On one side of them was Secret Agent Alex Crane, Spy Force's top spy, with their newest agent, Suave, whilst on the other was Steinberger. His head had been bandaged and several bandaids plastered his arms and hands.

'Last night, Quimby, Plomb, and Steinberger were targeted by what we believe to be the main spam.' Harrison paused. 'I of course mean the *same man.*'

Eleanor breathed in a small gasp. 'Is everyone OK?'

'Apart from a few cuts and bruises, yes, thankfully they are.'

Max clutched her backpack to her chest and looked towards Steinberger, who had moved to the back of the room to set up a projector and laptop. He concentrated intently on the equipment, acting as if nothing had happened.

'A professional killer?' Linden's skin prickled all over when he said it out loud.

'We believe so,' Harrison confirmed.

'Do you know who it is?' Ben asked.

'A man named Andriya Sorenson.'

Alex and Suave got their palm computers out, ready to take notes as Steinberger pressed a button on the projector's remote and brought to life an image of the killer's face on the screen in front of them. He had shoulder-length blond hair and ice-blue eyes, with finely chiselled cheeks, nose, and jaw line.

'He's a contract killer who is active in countries all over the world.'

'A contract killer?' Max felt as if she'd swallowed a marble. 'If he's known, how come he hasn't been caught?'

'He makes it very difficult for anyone to find him,' Suave said, offering Max a warm smile. The last time they'd seen each other was after their mission in the Amazon, when Suave was thinking of leaving the Force due to an uncontrollable fear of worms. Even though Max hadn't liked him at first,* he was a good agent and she was glad he'd changed his mind.

'Take a look at this,' Harrison instructed.

Steinberger pressed the remote again. The screen filled with a black and white photo of a man stepping onto a yacht, his head turned, as if watching his back.

'This one was taken on a wharf in Zanzibar off the East African coast. He was being followed by one of our agents who, after months of undercover work, had tracked him down.'

The photo was slightly blurred, but the heavy features, rounded paunch, thick black moustache and wavy hair of the man were clear.

'Is that someone who works with him?' Linden guessed.

'No,' Harrison corrected, 'it's Sorenson.'

Max and Linden tried to see the resemblance between this man and the blond man they'd seen before.

'That wasn't his best. Look at this one.' Harrison nodded towards Steinberger.

This time, the image of a crowded marketplace appeared.

* See Max Remy Spy Force: The Amazon Experiment

'This is a street in the Austrian town of Kleinhattenberg,' Harrison said.

Max studied the picture. 'This guy is good. That looks like a real nun.'

Harrison looked at Max. 'She is a real nun. Look behind her.'

Apart from the sound of the projector fan, there was silence as each agent studied the picture. There was a butcher's shop, a flower stall, clusters of clothes racks, and a barrow packed with cheeses.

'There!' Linden pointed. 'He's the street performer.'

Amongst the milling shoppers and sellers, they saw him. A tall, thin man dressed in tights, with a whitened face and heavily coloured red lips.

'He has the same looking-over-his-shoulder expression he had on the yacht.'

Harrison smiled. 'Well done, Linden. Sorenson is not only an expert of disguise but of language as well, and as he has no fixed address, he is very difficult to pat down . . . I mean, *track down*.'

'We've been close to capturing him on several occasions,' Alex said pointedly. 'But he's managed to disappear just before capture. He works alone, has no ties, and when he has killed, he leaves no traces it was him or clues as to where he is going next.'

'It's as if he becomes invisible,' Harrison concluded.

'If he's so good,' Max frowned, 'how come none of the agents are . . .' She couldn't say the word sitting on the edge of her lips.

'Because he didn't intend to kill them,' Harrison answered. 'Take a look at this.'

It was a photo of Blue standing on a podium in front of a well-dressed dinner crowd. Even though they'd had news of his death, his face was still enough to drive a shiver into Max.

'This was taken a few months ago, before Blue's imprisonment. Here he's being honoured by the Royal Humanitarian Society.'

'Anyone told them yet they got the wrong man?' Linden asked.

'Look closely at the bottom right-hand corner of the screen,' Harrison continued.

Steinberger zoomed in. There was a table at the back of the room, swathed in darkness, and standing behind it was a man with his arms folded. He was dressed in a tuxedo, wore thick glasses beneath a balding head, and had that same guarded, over-his-shoulder look.

'Sorenson?' Max asked.

'Yes. After photographic analyses were conducted

on all four images, Quimby has confirmed that the man in each picture is Sorenson.'

'So Sorenson was working with Blue?' Eleanor shivered at the idea of two such devious minds working together.

'We believe it is here that Blue's relationship with Sorenson started to take shape,' Alex informed them.

Linden stepped towards the screen to take a closer look at the killer's disguise. It was good. 'But if Blue is dead, why is Sorenson doing this?'

Harrison's brow bulged into a complex tangle of lines, as if there wasn't enough room for all the thoughts crammed into his head. 'Before he was attacked Steinberger received a disk containing a message that was recorded yesterday.'

Harrison nodded to Steinberger, who slid a disk out of a round cover and placed it in his computer. A startling image appeared before them.

It was Blue. Thinner than his usual self but with the same self-satisfied grin he wore for his most victorious moments.

'But he's dead?' Max said more as a question.

'So we thought,' Harrison replied.

'It must have been filmed before the fire,' Ben suggested.

'Locked within the digital code of the disk is

the time it was recorded,' Suave added. 'Which was several hours after the fire took place.'

'So it's really him?' Eleanor spoke softly.

'We still have Blue's Vibratron reading from his days at the Force, which confirms the fingerprint-like identification of his vibrations,' said Alex.

'You can measure those vibrations from a digital image?' Linden was amazed.

'With Quimby's Vibrations Decoder we can, yes, and it is an identical match.'

Max felt deflated. It was getting harder to know what was real and what wasn't.

'It's either him or a very good copy.' Steinberger pressed play, causing the image of Blue to come to life.

'I thought it was time we all had a little chat.' Blue's voice reverberated around them. 'I'm assuming you are all there after being summoned by your gracious leader and, like good little minions, you have responded to the call.'

Ben flinched. Seeing Blue's face again brought back all the lies Blue had told Ben while they worked together at the Department of Science and New Technologies.*

* See *Max Remy Spy Force: The Time and Space Machine*

'Bravo on your little plan to put me away like some common criminal after our short time together in the Amazon, but I'm afraid it will take much more to keep me locked away.' Blue sniffed. 'As you all know, I am dead, or so the world thinks. Terrible fire it was, and such a tragedy to die after all I did to save the lives of my fellow inmates. To reach death with such valour is truly heroic, don't you think? Anyway, enough of my bravery, you'll want to know why I have orchestrated my own death. I won't tell you how,' he spat with particular disgust. 'You're the top spy agency, you work it out. For now, this is my request: it is time you and I met, Harrison, for a little chat at one of my properties. The details of which I'll tell you once you have accepted my invitation.'

The look in Blue's eyes made Max realize that if Harrison did meet him, he might never return.

'You will find a number on the upper side of this disk that can only be revealed under UV light. It is a direct line to me.' He smiled a salivating smile. 'I would hate for you not to accept, for who knows what other accidents may befall those around you.'

Ben flinched in anger. 'So it was him who attacked the agents.'

'But how could Blue be dead and then send a

message?' Linden was trying to understand what was going on. 'The guards at Blacksea had his body in the morgue.'

'Quimby is working on ideas of how it could be possible.' Suave looked up from his palm computer. 'She believes she's close and will have the answer soon.'

'What's the security situation here?' Ben knew it would be good but he needed to know Blue had no chance of getting any closer to Spy Force than he was in that recording.

'We recently changed the security fields around the complex and will do so every twenty-four hours.' Harrison looked at Max and Linden. 'It's like changing the locks on a house as well as moving it to a new location. It's very safe.'

'We will do everything we can to keep Spy Force HQ and agents safe.' Alex looked at Max for the first time since they had arrived, offering an almost smile. One that seemed to promise to Max in particular that she would be safe.

'There is one more thing.' Harrison had been saving the hardest news for last. 'Max, we know where your mother is.'

Max felt as if her breath had been forced out of her in one painful punch.

'The readings came through identifying the men in the helicopter. One is a known ally of Blue. The other was Sorenson.' Harrison held out a folded piece of paper. 'And there's this. It was an attachment we printed out from the disk.'

Max was unable to move, afraid of what it might contain.

Linden took it and handed it to her, whispering, 'We're all here for you, Max.'

She gulped a steadying breath and cautiously took the paper.

When she opened it out, she saw a photo. It took whole seconds to make sense of what she saw. The room began to waver around her and she felt herself falling like a parachutist into a cloud. She slumped slowly down into the sofa and saw the photo fall from her fingers and float to the floor.

'Max?' Eleanor rushed from her sofa and knelt beside her niece. She picked up the photo and felt sick at what she saw.

It was a picture of Max's mother. She was standing in a darkened room, her hands clasping the iron bars of a prison cell. She was still wearing her wedding dress, which looked dirty and torn. On the back was a scribbled message that said:

Wish you were here,
Love Mum

'Where is she?' Max wanted what she was seeing not to be true.

'With Blue,' Harrison answered quietly.

'What is he playing at?' Ben was furious.

'Revenge mostly,' Harrison explained. 'But there are other reasons he has yet to make clear to us.'

'Revenge? What has my mother ever done to him?' Max could feel the blood racing through her veins as her fury rose.

'We've yet to work that out but, with respect, Max, it's not about your mother. Or Steinberger, Quimby, or Plomb. Blue likes to savour his revenge by working towards his main target through those around them.'

'His main target?' Linden looked puzzled.

'Me.'

Max and Linden fell into a breathless silence.

'He has wanted his revenge on me for years for kicking him out of the Force and now he aims to get it.'

Linden glanced at Max and knew he was ready to do anything to save her mother. 'What should we do now?'

'I've accepted Blue's invitation.'

'But, sir . . . ?' Steinberger's head shot up. 'If something were to happen to you . . .'

'Sir,' Alex spoke frankly, 'you will be walking into a trap. One that Blue will not let you escape from.'

It was obvious Harrison had wanted to make his announcement without any discussion.

'Max's mother needs our help and . . .' Here Harrison's voice gave away a deeper, hidden level of anger. '. . . I will not let Blue toy with Spy Force agents any longer. If he wants to have his revenge on me, let him have his chance.'

His words were edged with defiance. 'Agents Crane and Suave?'

Alex paused only momentarily. 'We stand by your decision, sir.'

'Absolutely, sir,' Suave added.

'Steinberger? Do I have your support?'

Steinberger stared at Harrison. He dreaded the outcome of his decision, but his loyalty and trust towards the Chief of Spy Force far outweighed that dread.

'Completely, Mr Harrison.'

Max's mouth went dry as she listened. How could they agree with him? Harrison was a brilliant leader and he had been a great spy when he was young, but once Blue had him where he wanted him, it would be a fight that would not be over until someone was dead.

'Sir, why don't you send . . .'

Max was interrupted by beeping from Harrison's computer. He looked down at the screen and activated the message link. It was Quimby.

'Sir, we have the answer to Blue's apparent double existence. A few years ago Blue was working on a Doppelgänger, a device capable of creating perfect human replicas. You may remember that after the ramifications of such a device were explored, your father, then head of Spy Force, refused to let the experiments continue. The project was cancelled and all the research was destroyed.'

'A doppelgänger?' Linden marvelled at such a device. 'And it creates an exact replica of a human?'

'That was his aim while he worked here,' Quimby replied.

'So the replica of Blue was the one who saved the prisoners from the fire. And the one who was killed,' Eleanor spelt out for them. 'Which leaves Blue to do his dirty work as freely as he likes, without anyone knowing it's him.'

'Thanks, Quimby. I'll be down to be equipped immediately.' Harrison shut down his computer and stood up from his desk.

'Should we be equipped too, sir?' Max asked as she and Linden leapt from their sofa.

Suave gave Alex a sideways glance before looking back at his notes. It was a look that told Max she wasn't going to like what Harrison had to say.

'Max, we can't allow you to be on this mission.'

Ben and Eleanor looked at each other, familiar with this Spy Force rule.

'Sorry?'

Harrison fixed Max with a steadfast eye. 'You're too close to this one, Max. Your emotional involvement in this mission may well cause you to jeopardize its outcome.'

'But that's crazy!' Max raised her voice. 'She's my mother. I know her the best and I'm a good spy. I'm the perfect one to be on this mission.'

Harrison looked at her as she calmed down from her outburst. 'It is exactly that kind of emotion that can cost lives.'

He walked over to her, gently laying his hands on her shoulders. 'Max, you are one of the most courageous and skilled spies I've ever known, but in this instance, I refuse to let you go on this mission. You are welcome to stay with Steinberger, Alex, and Suave, who will oversee the operation from here, or you can go home and we will keep you informed of everything that happens.'

'But, sir . . .'

'My decision is final, Max.' His words ended with a resounding full stop and Harrison left the room with the weight of his decision riding on his heels.

Max stared after him, desperate to stop him, to have him change his mind. As he walked out of the door she knew she couldn't let him go on this mission alone. She had to find her mother, and even Spy Force wasn't going to stop her.

CHAPTER 11
A SNEAKY THEFT AND SOME DEVASTATING NEWS

Max stood before the solid stone structure of the Wall of Goodness. She clenched her hands into nervous fists and looked across at Linden.

'Are you sure you're OK about doing this?'

'Sure I'm sure.'

Linden finished off the last of a sesame seed bar, put the wrapper in his backpack and stared at the Wall.

'But we're going against Harrison's orders.'

'We're going to rescue your mum,' Linden replied easily. 'Anyway, rules and orders only matter as long as they don't get in the way of what's right. And yes, before you ask, that was another one of Mum's sayings.'

Max smiled. 'Was there anything your mum didn't have a saying for?'

Linden thought about it. 'Nope. Now, time to go in, eh? Oh, and Max?' He prepared to give her one last piece of advice. 'Try to get it right this time, will you?'

Max grimaced. She'd never once been through the Wall of Goodness without some kind of spluttering, gurgling trouble. The Wall was created to let only true and honest people through to the heart of the Force. It had never yet failed to do its job, and even though Max knew what they were doing was right, she wasn't so sure the Wall would feel the same.

They stood perfectly still, as Steinberger had instructed them in the past, and stared straight ahead. Within seconds the Wall's atoms began reconfiguring as it went into identification mode. It reached out and began enveloping them with a warm, custardy ooziness, massaging Max and Linden to assess their level of Goodness.

'See you on the other side,' Linden winked.

But then, the Wall's kneading slowed down until it had almost stopped.

'It's not going to let us through,' Max said despairingly. She knew that at that moment Harrison was in Quimby's lab being equipped for his mission, and if they didn't get through soon he'd be gone, along with their hopes of following him.

'Please, Wall,' she said softly. 'We've got to get in or . . .'

Before she could finish, the Wall came to life again with even more force than before, and after a final, heaving lurch, it totally enveloped them in one squelching slurp.

In Quimby's lab, the Wall spat Max out in a stumbling, arm-flinging stop, but for Linden it was more like a gentle shove.

'Max? Linden? I didn't know you were coming down.' Quimby stood at her workbench beside rows of shelves and cupboards filled with Spy Force devices, puzzled by the sudden appearance of the two young spies.

Max shot Linden a quick look signalling she'd take care of the explanation.

'We wanted to make sure you were feeling OK after last night and wish Mr Harrison good luck for his mission.'

Quimby blushed. 'I'm fine, thank you. My cat Millie's a little nervy but it's nothing her super-confidence can't conquer.'

Harrison seemed a little miffed that they had followed him.

'Your decision was to stay with Steinberger or go home.'

'I'm not very good at sitting still since Mum . . .' Max couldn't finish.

Harrison softened. 'Max, you needn't worry, I will be fried.'

This time it was Max, Linden, and Quimby who flinched at their leader's word fumble.

'You mean *fine*, we know,' Max corrected. 'And you will be.'

'We'd better keep preparing for the mission,'

Quimby said softly. 'And, Max, I'm sorry about your mother. We will find her, you know that?'

Max nodded.

Quimby turned to a cupboard behind her and picked up a small piece of cloth that folded out to a lightweight bodysuit. 'This is an Impact Suit. It fits snugly on the body and works much like a suit of armour, a bullet-proof vest, and an airbag at the same time. It is made from the toughest yet softest material and is lined with a slim hyper-strong gel that absorbs all the impact of a hit or fall. It's also an excellent buoyancy vest.'

Quimby placed the suit on her work-bench alongside a line of other compact gadgets she'd prepared for Harrison.

'Now to your new jacket.' She held up a coat identical to the one Harrison was wearing. 'The second button down is a miniature camera, two-way radio, and location device. As your last communication with Blue instructed you to turn up unarmed and unaccompanied, I thought this would be the most discreet way of staying in touch.'

She laid the jacket on the bench and picked up a coin-shaped object.

'Finally we have the Undetectatron, a very clever device that creates a force-field of energy around you so that you are completely unnoticeable to any security devices you come across. Simply remove the label from the back and stick the device to your chest and it is activated. You won't need it at first as Blue will be expecting your arrival, but it will be handy if you need to make an unseen escape.'

She smiled proudly at the array of gadgets before them. 'All we need to do now, sir, is take you to the lab's changing rooms to attach the Undetectatron, get you fitted into your Impact Suit, and you will be ready to go.'

'Excellent.' Harrison turned to Max and Linden. 'You two better get back to Steinberger.'

'Would you mind, sir, if we saw you off?'

Max's heart lurched at Harrison's hesitation.

'OK, but as soon as I leave, you are to stick very closely to Ben and Eleanor. I want them to know where you are at all times.'

'Absolutely, sir.'

Max hated lying to Harrison, but now that her plan to save her mother had begun, she couldn't turn back.

After Harrison and Quimby walked into the next room, Max and Linden sprang towards Quimby's cupboards and selected their gadgets.

'We'll need Danger Meters, these Undetectatrons should be useful, and I like the sound of those suits. And this . . .' Linden grabbed an X-ray Spectrogram like the one he and Max had used in Morocco. '. . . might be good too.'

As they put the devices into their packs, Max felt better now that she was doing something active about saving her mother.

'What about when Quimby notices what's missing?' Linden asked.

'She doesn't check her equipment until the end of each day. By then, we'll be a long way from here.' But Max knew what Linden was getting at. 'When we get back from the mission with Mum and Harrison safe, she'll understand why we did it.'

Linden smiled. 'We've already got our Personal Flying Devices in our packs, so what else do we need?' He looked around. 'What about this?' He took a pen from a drawer that said 'Knock Out Spray'.

'Great. And look at these.' Max spied a velvet-lined box with jewelled rings inside. They were all different shapes and colours, and attached to the shelf they sat on was a card that said 'Digital Camera and Laser Rings'. She slipped one into her pocket just as they heard Quimby's and Harrison's voices coming closer.

She quickly closed the cupboard doors and drawers and they both leant against Quimby's workbench as if they'd been patiently waiting for their return.

'Good luck, sir,' Quimby offered.

'Thank you, Quimby. You're a wonderful asset to the Force.'

Quimby tucked a falling piece of hair into her scarf and blushed.

Max, Linden, and Harrison made their way to the VART. As Max followed her leader, she knew there was one more thing she needed. The location of the meeting.

Harrison had decided not to use the Time and Space Machine as it would be too risky to have it so close to Blue. Instead, he had arranged to be flown to a large open field in the north of Scotland, where he would be picked up, blindfolded, and taken to his destination.

As they walked down the metal boardwalk of the VART, Alex, Suave, Ben, and Eleanor were waiting to say farewell to their chief, while Steinberger was on the hangar floor, showing Sleek a map.

Max took a hanky from her pocket and brought it to her nose, carefully concealing the digital camera ring. Linden threw her a subtle smile as she zoomed in on the map and took several photos.

Steinberger stepped towards the main group and Max put her hanky and the ring back in her pocket.

'Everything has been prepared just as you requested, sir.' Steinberger tried to keep his voice firm. He held out an overcoat and hat. 'All available agents and vehicles are on standby if you need us, and the communication channels that connect you to Spy Force will be clear and operational at all times.'

'Excellent.' Harrison put on the coat and hat.

'Quimby is certain your jacket button locator will let us know your exact position once you have arrived,' Alex added confidently.

Harrison turned towards his ride, which was the Sleek Machine. It was a cross between a motorbike and a glider, and moved at an oscillation level that made it and its passengers invisible.

Sleek sat on the main body of the machine dressed in a long leather coat, warm hat, and thick-lensed goggles. He handed Harrison a second pair of goggles. The chief put them on and climbed into the attached sidecar.

'Sir.' Max rushed to the machine. 'Is there

really no way we can come? Linden and I could be ready in minutes if you thought . . .'

Harrison locked on to her eager expression with a look that cut her enthusiasm short. 'I'm sorry, Max.'

'OK.' She moved away slightly. 'I understand.'

Eleanor stepped forward and put her hands on Max's shoulders. 'Please come back safely,' she said to Harrison. 'Both you and my sister.'

Harrison nodded and Sleek started the engine. When the machine lifted into the air towards the exit of the VART, it disappeared, leaving only the sound of the engine fading into the distance.

Steinberger, Suave, and Alex excused themselves and went to resume their part of the mission. Eleanor gently turned Max towards her and took her hands. 'Let's get you something to eat, shall we?'

Max felt bad about needing to keep their rescue plans secret from her aunt and uncle, but she couldn't risk them stopping her. She turned away from Eleanor, a heavy sadness slumped into her shoulders. 'I'll meet you in the canteen. I think I just want to wait here for a little while if that's OK.'

'Of course it's OK,' Ben said with a swooping hug. 'You take all the time you need, and I'll get Irene to whip up something extra special.' But when he let her go, Max could see he didn't want to leave her alone.

'Linden, can you stay with me?'

'Sure.' Linden stepped forward.

'We'll see you both in the canteen.' Eleanor reached for Ben's hand and they walked out of the VART. Ben turned for a last glance at his niece and gave a small wave.

Max waved back and watched as they disappeared from view.

'It's OK, Max.' Linden guessed her thoughts. 'When they know why we did it, they'll be OK.'

'I know it's risky but I can't just sit here and do nothing any more.' Max sat on the floor. 'You don't have to come if you don't want to. I'd understand,' she said, even though she knew that without him she might not make it back.

Linden sat down beside her. 'How long should we wait before we follow Harrison?'

'Best to give him a head start, then we'll follow from a safe distance.' Max paused. 'I know Harrison thought using the Time and Space Machine was risky around Blue, but we've done it before. I know we can keep it safe. And besides, with our Undetectatrons on, I'm not planning for Blue to even know we're there.'

She took out her palm computer and the digital camera ring. She plugged the ring into the top USB port and within seconds an image of the map she had photographed appeared before her. 'It's done a good job.'

Max activated the locator in the computer to give her the coordinates of where Steinberger was pointing. Within seconds she had them. 'Latitude 58 degrees 37 seconds north and longitude 5 degrees west.' Max's joy at having found the meeting point then faded. 'Oh.'

'What's wrong?'

'The name of the place Harrison is going to is Cape Wrath.'

'It's just a name,' Linden suggested, but he too was nervous about what it might mean.

Max took the ring from the computer and put it on her finger, knowing they might need it later. She then felt a shiver run through her and rubbed her arms. 'Do you feel cold?'

'Kind of. Maybe it's just nerves.'

'Or maybe . . .'

'What are you kids doing here?'

Max knew that voice and the reason for her sudden chill. Dretch. Her heart jolted in a breathless panic. She turned off her palm computer and slipped it into her pocket, hoping Dretch had not seen what she had just been doing.

His footsteps came closer as he walked along the metal boardwalk towards them. His dislike for Max and Linden had been clear from the moment they first arrived at Spy Force. If he found out what they were doing, Max knew he would have great pleasure in demanding they be thrown off the Force.

'Thought you were supposed to be with Ben and Eleanor?' He now stood above them and, Max realized with horror, his eyes were focused on the digital camera ring. His eyebrows curved upwards and Max knew they were caught.

She jumped up, desperate to explain. 'We were, but . . .'

Dretch cut her off. 'I have something for you.'

'For me?' Max could almost hear the crack of icy Dretch vibes spilling all over her.

He handed her a memory stick. Max took out the small rectangular device and stared up at the scarred face of the man standing beside her. 'Um, thanks.'

She was hoping this would be the end of their conversation and the beginning of him turning away and leaving, but Dretch stayed where he was and just kept staring. What was he waiting for, Max thought, a hug?

The air thickened around them. The chill sank into her bones even further.

'Aren't you going to look at it?'

There was something bossy but soft about Dretch that was hard to understand. And now that he'd seen the ring and knew Max shouldn't have it, why wasn't he saying anything about it?

'Oh. Yeah.'

'It was at the end of the disk Blue sent,' Dretch said awkwardly. 'The others thought it would be too upsetting for you, but I thought you should know.'

Max and Linden had a bad feeling about what they were about to see.

Max took out her palm computer and plugged in the memory stick. The image of a darkened room appeared before them. 'It's the picture of Mum.'

As Max whispered the words, her mother called out.

'You can't keep me in here! Do you hear me? As soon as the police find out where I am, you will be spending the rest of your miserable, brain-dead days in a prison much worse than this.'

'Mum,' Max said quietly. 'Don't upset them.'

The image then pulled away as if the camera was backing down a long corridor. Max's mother kept up her angry abuse. Then there was an explosion. Max flinched as if she'd been hit. The image filled with smoke and flying bits of debris. Then it went black.

They stared at the computer. Dretch's hands made fists in his coat pockets, clenching and unclenching. His lips moved as if he was trying to speak.

'Max?' Linden said gently.

A dull, greyish colour filled Max's face.

Dretch looked quickly between the two young spies.

'Max?' Linden wanted her to say something, do something. Anything but keep quiet.

'I think I'm going to be sick.'

Dretch caught the palm computer that flew from Max's hands as she ran from the VART into the closest bathroom.

Linden ran after her and pushed open the door.

'Max!' His voice echoed around the tiled room. 'Max? Are you in here?'

He looked in all the cubicles until he saw Max huddled on the floor. Her hands cradled her knees, which were pulled tightly into her chest. Linden sat next to her and watched as the shock of what she'd just seen sank into her. She felt as if she was in a nightmare she couldn't wake from.

The door of the toilets creaked open and Dretch slunk in with his head down, so that his spaghetti fringe dipped over his scarred face more than usual.

'I . . . ah . . . I . . .' he mumbled.

Max started to cry. 'It can't be true, Linden. It can't be!'

Dretch stared at her folded body bobbing up and down with each sobbing breath. He watched as her tears made small circular stains on her suede trainers, her sniffles reverberating off the walls so they sounded even sadder.

'Remember, this is Blue,' Linden said firmly. 'What we see isn't always what is happening.'

Dretch took an awkward step towards Max but then stopped, unsure of what to do. His spindly fingers came out of his pocket and he reached over and patted her head.

'I think Linden's right,' he said gruffly. 'I worked with Blue long enough to know he's up to something, I just don't know what it is yet.'

Max wanted to disappear for ever from who she was and what she'd just seen.

'I want to go home.' Her voice fluttered around the room like a broken-winged butterfly, but after she'd said it, she realized she didn't have a home any more. Not now that her mother wasn't there.

Suddenly she had this itching, breathless need to run. To get away from Spy Force. To get away from what had happened.

She stood up as another wave of nausea swiftly came over her, but it was then she realized it wasn't being in or getting away from any one place that she needed. She needed to get away from what she'd just found out and, no matter where she went, she knew she never could.

CHAPTER 12
A MEETING OF OLD FRIENDS

The Sleek Machine swayed and lurched in the fury of thrashing winds tearing at the craggy coastline of Cape Wrath. The wind circled around them like a pack of howling wolves, biting into them with each ice-filled blast. Sleek held the controls firm as he negotiated each gusting push and shove that slammed into the machine, until he finally landed on the damp, rock-strewn ground.

Sleek took the goggles Harrison offered him and gave a sombre nod of farewell. A farewell, he knew, that might be their last. He adjusted his goggles before taking off into the sky, reaching his oscillation speed and disappearing seconds later.

Harrison looked around him at the gloomy horizon and pulled his overcoat tighter across his chest. A white mist whipped up from the freezing waves of the Atlantic Ocean smacked into him, leaving him cold and stinging.

'So this is where you live?' His lips moved slowly in the biting cold.

From over the horizon a four-wheel drive vehicle with thick, all-terrain tyres drove into view. It bumped over the gnarled and stony landscape before coming to an abrupt stop.

'Kronch. Of course,' Harrison murmured.

It always amazed Harrison that Blue kept

Kronch on as one of his henchmen, especially considering his brain was rarely used for thinking.

Kronch lifted his log-shaped legs and tennis racquet-sized shoes out of the vehicle with a concerted wheeze.

'Your lift awaits.' He swung his arm out as if he was a doorman at an expensive hotel.

Harrison climbed inside and strapped himself in, happy to be out of the gnawing wind. Kronch took a small device from his pocket and seemed to be taking a reading of the area.

'Well done. You're here alone. It's good to see you can follow orders when you want to,' Kronch snivelled as he squeezed his jellied belly behind the wheel.

Harrison knew it was a dig at his last days with Blue at Spy Force and the conflicting views of the two men when it came to running the agency. Harrison believed in a sense of honesty and fair play, whereas Blue couldn't see the harm in bending a few rules to make money. Selling Spy Force inventions to known criminals, for example. Inventions such as the Doppelgänger.

Harrison stared outside as the grey and brown landscape blurred past.

There was something else he noticed. Kronch

hadn't blindfolded him. He thought meeting at Cape Wrath was to conceal the real location of Blue's mansion, but here he was being driven there in murky daylight. It could mean Blue had a security system in place that Harrison could not hope to renegotiate if he returned. Or, and this second idea seemed more likely, Blue planned Harrison would never leave.

Kronch wrenched the steering wheel hard to the left, sending the vehicle ricocheting off a large rock before hitting the ground with a bouncing thud. Harrison dug his heels into the floor and gripped the armrest even tighter, refusing to be thrown around by Kronch's attempts to frighten him. He held firm and stared into the rear-view mirror, catching Kronch's thick-witted grin. Blue and his pack of brainless thugs could try to scare him all they liked. Harrison had no intention of letting them get to him, and he became even more determined in his refusal to be afraid.

The jolting ride continued up a slippery, mud-soaked hill, and it was only when they reached the top that the vision of Blue's property appeared before them.

Only his property turned out to be a castle.

Flanked by eight round towers joined by stone

curtained walls, the castle keep rose in the centre of the fortress, dominating not only the castle but also the windswept hill it rested on.

'This is it,' Kronch yelled into the wind, bringing the vehicle to an abrupt, screeching halt.

Harrison stepped out and watched as the car drove off in a shower of rocks and mud. He walked towards the entrance of the castle but stopped as he reached the deep, cold moat, snaking around the ancient building and licking its algae-stained walls. It looked dismal and dark. As he was about to turn away, something in the moat moved, breaking the icy surface in an angry splash, as if lashing out against being there.

The drawbridge then began to slowly lower towards him. On either side of the rough, splintered bridge, great iron chains slowly unwound in a yawning, screaming creak, as if the souls of a thousand dead had risen to welcome guests who entered.

The drawbridge finally slammed into the ground with a dull, exhausted thud. Harrison squinted into the dim arched entranceway and saw a figure walk from the shadows.

'Welcome.' Blue strode across the bridge in his immaculately polished shoes. He looked smug and lordly, delighted to be able to show off his not-so-humble home.

'Sorry about the weather. It's unusual to be so chilly at this time of year.'

Harrison plunged his hands deeper into his pockets. 'I haven't come all this way to talk about the weather, Theodoran.'

Blue was disappointed that Harrison didn't seem more impressed, but immediately recovered his arrogance. He straightened his back and flicked his head in a superior gesture. 'I knew all I needed was to create the right conditions and you'd come running.'

'Well, I'm here now and I don't plan on staying long.'

A creepy smile slithered onto Blue's lips.

'Oh, but there's so much to talk about. All those old times. You and I, side by side, working together to create the greatest agency the world had ever seen.'

An angry gust of wind bullied its way between the two men.

'We may have been physically side by side,' Harrison said, at pains to make his views clear, 'but our ideas on what made an agency great were never closely aligned.'

'Come now. You know you wanted exactly what I wanted . . . it was simply our methods that varied in a few minor ways.'

Harrison had finished talking about the past and wanted Blue to know it.

'What is it you want, Theodoran?'

'Ah, still the same old Harrison, I see. Straight down to business.'

Harrison held his gaze firm, refusing to buy into any of Blue's games.

'Let's get out of the cold, shall we?' Blue suggested casually. 'We can discuss matters further in more comfortable surroundings.'

Blue stood aside, inviting Harrison into the dark interior of the castle. Their footsteps reverberated off the stone floor, echoing around their heads into the shadowy corners of the lofty ceilings. Behind them, the screeching crank of winding chains drew the heavy wooden drawbridge to a booming close.

CHAPTER 13

A HARD DECISION

The Time and Space Machine flung Max, Linden, Ben, and Eleanor through space so quickly that, in a matter of seconds, they were transported from Spy Force HQ in London to Max's lounge room in Sydney. In a flash of fluorescent light they hovered momentarily in the air before floating gently to the floor.

Max recoiled, taking a sudden deep breath. She had known it would be hard to come home, but now that she was actually here, it felt as if she'd been punched hard in the chest.

When Dretch alerted Ben and Eleanor about what he'd told Max, they immediately hurried to the toilets and found her slumped in Linden's arms, crying. Ben carefully picked her up and Eleanor wrapped her in a sweeping shawl.

Ben softly lifted Max's chin and looked intently into her eyes. 'I'm not ready to believe anything that comes from Blue. Remember that. And now we're going to get you home, where we can take proper care of you and wait to see what has really happened.'

Max nodded her head lifelessly and after a brief and sad goodbye to Steinberger, they had left.

'Let me get that for you.' Linden leant across and took off Max's backpack. Normally she would have told him she could do it herself, but today she lowered her shoulders with a listless, resigned slouch, letting the backpack slide off into Linden's waiting hands.

The apartment was still overrun with unopened wedding presents, baskets of fruit, boxes of chocolates, flowers and cards, so that it looked like a party where no one had turned up. It only made Max feel sadder.

Ben kept looking at a drawn and pale Eleanor, as if he was scared she was going to break, and Linden was never far from Max's side. They hadn't slept for over twenty-four hours. They hadn't been able to. Just closing their eyes filled their minds with the same terrible images.

No one knew what to say or do. It seemed everything they thought of was trivial and unimportant compared to what had happened.

'Max, love, can I get you anything?' Ben stared at her anxiously.

'No thanks, Ben. I think I'll go to my room.'

Max started climbing the stairs. Ben couldn't stand the idea of her being alone. 'How about we make up a bed for Linden on your floor? Would you like that?'

'Sure.' Max paused. 'We should tell Dad. And Aidan.'

'We'll wait until we know for certain what has happened.' Eleanor had seen the tape too, and although she felt despair at what she'd seen, she too wasn't ready to believe anything that had come from Blue.

After Eleanor and Ben had made up a makeshift bed for Linden on Max's floor, they closed the curtains, kissed both of them and left the bedroom.

Max's bed was normally so soft and comfortable that one of her favourite parts of the day was sinking into it, but now it felt big and cold, and no matter how much she snuggled in, she couldn't get warm.

Linden lay on his back on the floor, the reading lamp throwing a soft glow over both of them.

'Linden?'

'Yeah?'

'I don't want to do this any more.'

'What?' He held his breath and felt his body tense all over.

Then she said it. The thing Linden had dreaded most.

'Be in Spy Force.'

Linden turned over to face Max. 'Sure you can. You just don't feel like it now. Later on when this is all sorted out, it'll be different.'

'No,' Max whispered. 'I can't.'

The way she said it made Linden feel as if he'd lost his footing and fallen over the edge of a deep ravine.

'I . . . I . . .' Max knew what she had to say but every ounce of her was trying to resist it. 'I can't be a spy any more.'

'But, Max, you're a great spy. A real natural. You've worked so hard . . . and look at all the things you've learnt, like . . .'

'Like this business is too dangerous, and if you stay long enough you lose.'

There was a grinding pause between them.

'I almost lost my dad and you, and now I've lost my . . .' She tried to steel herself for the rest of what she had to say. 'Look at Alex. She lost her dad. And Dretch, he was a top spy before the accident on his last mission, and now he's a maintenance operator. Plomb was nearly blown up and Quimby and Steinberger aren't even safe in their own homes.'

Linden sat up. He felt as if he was in a whirlpool, sinking, about to be swallowed up. He had to make Max change her mind.

'At first I thought it was great,' Max went on. 'When I wrote my spy stories, I'd take on the bad guys and defeat them and the world would be a safer place . . . But it's not safe. It's a world where people die and get kidnapped and buildings with your mum in them explode. Why didn't I see that before?'

She gasped from the effort of what she'd said. It was true. Knowing she was the cause of her mother's kidnapping and possibly her death, Max had lost the one thing that made her want to fight crime. The knowledge that, no matter what happened, somehow Spy Force could make it all right again. If what she had seen on the memory stick was true, this time there was no one who could make things right ever again.

'And, Linden, there's something else . . .'

'What's that?'

'Since Mum was kidnapped, I haven't been able to get a clear picture of her in my head. I try to see her in my mind but it's like an old photo that's out of focus. And when I do remember times we had together, all I can remember are the bad ones. The times when we yelled at each other or fought, or when I said really mean things to her.' She drew in a quick breath. 'I'm scared, Linden. What if she really is dead and I can never say sorry for all the times I was horrible? What if I can never tell her that she's a really great mum and I'm so proud of her because she's smart and strong and . . .' She gasped again as tears salted her cheeks. 'I really love her.'

Linden looked at Max's shaking shoulders. He stood up, sat on the edge of her bed and put his arms around her. Her whole body trembled and Linden just held her and let her cry.

When she had settled a little, she wiped her eyes on her sleeve. 'Sorry. It must sound silly, huh?'

Linden gave Max a half-smile. 'It doesn't sound silly. I think about those kind of things every day.'

Max had been so caught up in her sadness she'd forgotten about Linden's mum.

'It's almost three years since Mum died and I still have things I want to tell her. Especially if I feel sad.'

'So what do you do?' Max sniffed.

'I tell her anyway. She's always listening.' He looked down and let loose a small, crooked smile. 'She had the best hearing of anyone I know. No matter where I was, if I mumbled or complained about something, she'd hear me. I could be whole rooms away in the house or even in the yard and she'd still hear. Never worked out how she did it.'

'How do you stop missing her?'

'I don't. It just doesn't hurt as much as it did.

At first I was really angry. Angry at everyone and anything. Angry at the doctors because they couldn't cure her cancer, angry at Dad for not talking to me, angry at myself for not taking better care of her when she was here.'

Max couldn't imagine Linden angry with anyone.

'And you know what, I couldn't remember what she looked like either. I'd lie awake at night and try to remember things we did, homework we'd sat over, holidays we went on. I'd sneak old photo albums into my room and look at them, trying to remember.'

'What did you do?'

'Cried a lot at first. I don't remember much else. Then eventually it all came back. Little things at first. Her laugh, a few jokes she'd told me, times when I'd fallen asleep lying on her lap while she read me stories. It was all there in my head. I guess I just had to get over being so sad about it.'

Linden looked up briefly at Max and even though her hair was messy and her eyes were red and puffy, he thought she looked pretty.

'Max, can I tell you something?'

'Yeah.'

'I just want you to know that I . . . well . . . I really . . .'

The muffled sound of someone knocking on the front door filtered up from downstairs.

'Who's that?' Max slipped under the blankets.

Linden got up and put his ear against the door. He heard Eleanor talking to someone, but after a few minutes, the front door closed and it was quiet again.

'Whoever it was, it sounds like they didn't stay.'

Linden went back to his makeshift bed and, moments later, there was a knock on Max's door.

'Max, honey, it's your friend Toby. I told him you weren't feeling well but he really wants to see you,' Eleanor said softly.

'Toby?' she whispered to Linden. 'What's he doing here?'

Linden frowned. 'Not sure.' There was something about Toby being there that really annoyed him. 'You don't have to see him if you don't want to.'

Max sat up and gathered the blankets around her. 'No, it's OK.' She turned to the door. 'Come in.'

Toby walked in, dropped his bag on the floor and sat on the bed next to Max as if he did the same thing every day.

'I'll be downstairs if you need me.' Eleanor quietly closed the door.

'You really need to check your answering machine. I had a look as we passed it in the hallway and you have thirty-two messages.'

'Yeah, we've . . . um . . . we've been . . .' Max didn't know how to explain.

'We've been busy,' Linden said abruptly, staring at Toby as a warning for him to drop it.

Suddenly Toby became serious. 'I'm only joking, Max. I know what happened to your mum. It was all over the TV.'

He went quiet, checking to see if Max wanted to say anything, but she didn't.

'They said your mum's been kidnapped, but they wouldn't say why or who did it. At school today they wouldn't tell me where you were and when I called your mum's work, they wouldn't say anything about it.'

Still Max didn't speak.

Linden stood up, ready to show Toby out. 'I think it'd be better if you left.'

Toby ignored Linden's offer. 'What's going on, Max? I'm sorry for just barging in and I know you probably don't want me here, but I wanted to make sure you were OK and see if there's anything I could do.'

In the past, whenever Toby was this close to

her, Max would either get away from him as soon as she could or be ready with a verbal attack that was sharp and funny, but there was something in his voice Max had never heard before. Something that made her want to tell him everything.

Linden saw that look in her eyes and suddenly realized he didn't like how close Toby was sitting to Max. 'I can take you downstairs and we'll call you if—'

'Mum's been kidnapped by this guy who hates us because Linden and I are spies and we've ruined his plans on a few missions we did for this intelligence agency called Spy Force, only now it looks like he may have killed her.'

Toby didn't know whether to believe her or not. It sounded more like the plot of an action film than the life of the slightly weird girl in his class.

'Killed her?'

Now Linden really needed Toby to leave. 'Max is upset, Toby. She's not really making any sense right now.'

Linden knew they could use the Neuro Memory Atomizer to wipe Toby's memory of what Max had just told him, but to do that they'd need to tell Quimby why they needed it, and revealing Spy Force information to a non-Spy Force person could get Max kicked off the Force. And despite what Max had said about leaving, he had no intention of letting her quit, or get expelled.

'What are you going to do?'

Linden clenched his teeth as Toby put his hand on Max's knee.

'There's nothing I can do,' Max whispered.

'Is it true, Linden?' Toby turned to him. He looked sincere, but Linden didn't want to tell him anything.

'We don't know what's happening,' Linden said with an edge to his voice.

'But you can't just sit here. We have to do something.'

Max's palm computer beeped from her pack. 'Spy Force!' She reached in and grabbed the computer while Linden pulled Toby to the floor, out of sight of the computer's screen.

Max opened the connection and activated the message.

'Max? Err . . . ahem.'

Linden held his hand over Toby's mouth and watched as Max recoiled slightly from the computer.

'It's me, Dretch.' He moaned as if he was having trouble knowing what regular people did after they said hello. 'Ah . . . everything OK there?'

'Sort of. Not really,' Max replied.

Toby pulled Linden's hand away and whispered, 'Who's Dretch?'

Linden scowled and put his hand back. 'Someone you don't want to know.'

'No. Course not. Right. Well,' Dretch continued uneasily. 'I've been doing some thinking about your mum.'

'You have?' Max felt weird talking to Dretch. As if she'd suddenly decided it was a good idea to put her head in the mouth of a crocodile.

'Yeah. It's no secret I didn't think much of either of you two when you first came to the Force, but now, well, Harrison and Steinberger like you so there must be something good there.'

Linden's and Max's eyes met. This was probably the closest thing to a compliment they would ever get from Dretch.

'I don't think your mother's dead.'

Max's grip on her computer tightened. 'How do you know that?'

'There are a few things that don't add up.' His voice wheezed out of the speakers. 'I used to do data analysing when I was a young agent and I've analysed the recording of the . . . explosion . . . and there's a point within the digital coding of the tape where the pixellation becomes more like a computer-generated image than a recording of an actual event.'

Linden signalled to Toby to stay quiet as he moved next to Max and spoke to Dretch. 'At the point just before the explosion?'

'Exactly.'

'So . . .' Max needed to get it straight. 'The part we see of my mother standing at the bars of the cell is real but the rest never happened?'

'Seems how it is to me.'

'But why would Blue pretend she was dead?' The truth had been so mangled Max wasn't sure what to believe.

Dretch looked away and seemed to be having trouble getting ready to say the next bit. 'I think it's to get you both out of the picture.'

'Us?' Linden was confused.

'He wanted to hurt you, Max, so badly that you'd want to quit the Force. Linden, being so loyal, would follow, which would get rid of two of his most frustratingly successful foes.'

'We were being played like kids,' Max quietly fumed.

'Played, yes,' Dretch agreed. 'But not like kids.'

The idea that Max had wasted time coming back to Australia when her mother might still be alive and in danger ate into her so much that she wanted to smash things up and cry at the same time.

But she took a deep breath and did something else instead.

'I'm going to find her.'

Toby edged closer as Linden looked at Max. 'Are you sure?'

'Yes.'

'But we don't know where Blue is.'

'We do now.' Dretch mumbled. 'He's in a castle in the north of Scotland. Quimby has been leading a team to crack Blue's security shield, and with the help of the jacket's location device and X-ray Spectrogram, she's discovered his exact location as well as a layout of the castle's interior.'

'Are Alex and Suave going?' Max asked.

'They have been coordinating field agents in a major search for Sorenson, who we believe is in hiding awaiting further orders from Blue. Alex in particular is determined he won't cause any more damage or get away from them this time.'

'So no one has been sent to help Harrison and my mum?' she asked sadly.

'Harrison has given strict orders for no one to go after him until he gives the word.'

Max stared at the dour and scarred face of Dretch on the screen before her. She'd heard he was a brave and unconventional agent and had seen him win the Lifetime Achievement Award at the last Annual Spy Awards night,[*] but she still wasn't entirely sure she should trust him.

'Why are you telling us this?'

'It's no secret that on my last mission with Harrison, we didn't agree on strategy. Harrison insisted we follow his plan, which resulted in injuries that made me unable to continue as a field agent. I should have stood by what I thought was right, but I didn't. This time I am. Harrison being alone with Blue without back-up is a mistake.'

'Why didn't Steinberger tell me about my mother?' Max asked.

'He wanted to make sure it was true first. And he thinks you've been through enough without upsetting you again. He wasn't very happy with me when he found out I'd told you.'

'So Steinberger doesn't know you're talking to us?' Linden guessed.

[*] See *Max Remy Spy Force: The Nightmare Vortex*

'Not exactly. You know he's a stickler for rules . . . but sometimes a mission calls for rules to be broken,' Dretch said firmly. 'I believe a good agent acts on what they know, and we know that two people are in danger who need our help. And besides, I know you've broken a rule or two to complete your missions in the past.' He paused. 'You have good instincts. Trust them,' Dretch continued. 'And even though Harrison thinks you're too close to this mission, I think you're perfect for it.'

'So we should go?' Max asked.

'You need to do what you think is right,' Dretch answered firmly.

Max caught Toby's eager eye and suddenly knew what she had to do. 'We have to go and save them.'

Dretch looked through his spaghetti fringe and gave what could have been a smile, as if he had expected Max to come up with this answer all along. 'I have sent a map to your palm computers. It includes a layout of the grounds and the castle, and coordinates for the Time and Space Machine. Even though Harrison chose not to risk using the Time and Space Machine near Blue, time is against us so we have no choice. I've transported some gadgets to your destination using the Mini Transporter Capsule.

You'll find them in a small sack under a stunted tree on the clifftop where you land.'

'Got it.' Max felt herself move easily into action.

'Quimby has identified an unusual energy field in one of the sections of the castle. She's not sure what is causing it, but I have marked it out on the map as an area to avoid, at least until she works out what it is. And remember, no one except me knows you're going on this mission.' Dretch looked around as if he heard a sound behind him. 'Better go. Send me a message when you're there,' Dretch muttered, before fumbling with his computer and sending Max's screen blank.

'What was that all about?' Toby's eyes were on fire as he jumped up from the floor.

'Nothing. You already know too much,' Linden said abruptly.

'It's to do with that spy stuff you write about in your journal, isn't it, Max?' Toby had stolen Max's spy notebook at school and read it out loud during a fire drill.[*] 'And Spy Force. You wrote about Blue and gadgets and Time and Space Machines! So it's all true?'

[*] See Max Remy Spy Force: Spy Force Revealed

'You really have to leave.' Linden stood up and faced him squarely. 'Max and I need to be somewhere.'

'It is all true, isn't it?' Suddenly Toby looked struck. 'And we've done this before, haven't we? That's why I keep getting these images in my head of the three of us in weird places, like in the snow and in restaurants and an American film studio.'

Max knew there was no way she could deny it. Even though Toby's memory had been erased after their mission in Hollywood, it seemed bits were coming back to him.

Toby eyed Linden carefully. 'And if anyone's going to ask me to leave, I think it should be Max.'

Both boys turned to face her.

Max knew she had to make a decision fast. Toby could be annoying, but he was also really smart, and if it hadn't been for him being with them in Hollywood, they wouldn't have completed their mission and Linden would be dead. She also knew this might be the last time they'd spend together before he left to live in Europe, and that was the final thing that helped her decide.

'Can you leave straight away?'

Toby shot Linden a victory smile before

answering. 'I'll call Aunt Mabel and let her know I'm staying at a friend's place tonight.'

Toby picked up the phone on Max's desk while Linden gently pulled her aside. 'He doesn't have to come. You two don't even like each other.'

'I know, but Dretch said to trust my instincts and my instincts tell me we'll need him.'

Even though Linden was unhappy about it, it was obvious Max had made up her mind and wasn't about to change it.

'Should we tell Ben and Eleanor?' she asked.

Linden thought about it. They would worry if he and Max went missing, but they couldn't risk telling them in case they refused to let them go. 'Maybe just leave a note.'

Toby got off the phone. 'Everything's set. What do I do now?'

'Go downstairs, say goodbye to Eleanor and Ben and tell them that Linden and I are really tired and are having a sleep. Then meet us in the park at the end of the street. I'll tell you the rest from there.' Max pulled out a jumper and beanie from her drawer. 'And take these. It's going to be cold in Scotland.'

'Aye aye, captain.'

Toby left the room with a wink. Max began to

scribble a note to her aunt and uncle before she stopped. 'What if things go wrong? What if we never—'

'We'll be fine, Max. I know we will.'

As they both took their Impact Suits and Undetectatrons from their packs, Linden flashed Max a smile to drive away the worry from her eyes. Even though he knew they were good spies, he also knew that with everything that had happened on their previous missions, Blue wouldn't waste any chance he got at doing away with them once and for all.

CHAPTER 14
THE BATTLE LINES ARE DRAWN

'And this,' Blue explained with a small but self-important wave, 'is where all our most valuable experimentation takes place and inventions are created.'

Harrison peered down from the uppermost platform that circled the inner castle walls of Blue's cavernous laboratory. It was a curious mix of modern and ancient: a high-tech scientific lab, surrounded by the ancient stones and roughly chiselled stairs of an old and regal fortress.

'At present we have over three hundred different projects at various stages of completion, some of which are very exciting, I can assure you.'

Harrison watched the battalion of white-coated and masked technicians and scientists working with fierce concentration. He didn't let it show, but he quietly marvelled at the sophisticated technology and highly advanced equipment.

Kronch hovered behind the two men and sniggered while Blue smiled teasingly. 'I'll bet it would be a dream come true if Spy Force had access to even a smidgen of what you see before you now.'

The lab was good, but without the genius of Frond and Quimby, or the minds of Ben and Francis, who had invented the Time and Space

Machine, Harrison knew Blue's lab would never be as good as the one at Spy Force.

'If you're doing this to impress me, you're wasting your time.' Harrison's voice had an almost bored tone.

'Oh, Reginald, believe me, it has been a long time since I have felt the need to impress anyone. I am simply a student of science enjoying its many and varied wonders.'

'A student with a healthy streak of megalomania.'

Blue fixed Harrison in his gaze like a marksman lining up his target.

Harrison sighed. 'Why don't you just tell me why you have summoned me here.'

'No room for any fun, eh, Reginald? Just like always. But you are right, we are both very busy men.' Blue's eyes became alive with a renewed energy. 'As much as I resented your little attempt to lock me away in prison, it gave me a chance to think about my life and what I have done with it. I accept that there have been times when I deviated a little from what could be construed as the best of intentions, and as a result of my thinking, I am a changed man and now wish to alter the way I live.'

'You've changed your ways? And what about

your little plan to send Sorenson to attack Spy Force personnel?'

Blue's eyebrow twitched. 'Sorenson was a momentary slip into former bad habits that I assure you will not happen again.'

Harrison sniffed. 'Go on.'

'I know we have differed in the past about how to run an intelligence agency, but I finally see the sense of how you operate Spy Force . . . if only you could expand your operations, think of how much greater Spy Force could be.'

Harrison stared blankly into Blue's sincerity-coated look. 'So what is it you want?'

'I want you and me to work as a team again. With my resources and money and your brilliant team with its impeccable record, we could create the most profitable, efficient, and successful agency either of us could have ever dreamt of.'

Harrison was momentarily silent.

'You know, the trouble with you, Theodoran, is that you dangle things in front of your enemies that may make *you* leap and wag your tail, but simply hold no attraction for them.' Harrison again buried his hands into his jacket pockets and looked down at the lab. 'The one thing your offer does do is prove how very different we are.'

A venomous sneer worked its way onto Blue's lips while Harrison prepared for his final remark. 'Spy Force is one of the finest spy agencies in the world. You are right when you say we have an impeccable record, and I have no intention of tarnishing that now by joining forces with a man who has no idea about honesty, loyalty, or the fundamentals of what is right. No matter what offer you put in front of me, I will never work with your low and scheming ways. Is there anything else?'

The jovial Blue had been nudged aside by a Blue who simmered with anger. His body became rigid with fury. 'I have invited you into my home and all you do is insult me.' He sucked in a deep breath. 'And turn down an extraordinary offer you will never receive again.'

'I can live with that,' Harrison declared.

Blue tried to maintain his calm. 'Well, if you don't have the sense to join forces with me, are you at least interested in rescuing Max's squealing mother and in me calling off the orders to hurt your precious Spy Force agents?'

Harrison paused. 'I will do all I can to protect innocent people from you.'

'Now, at least, you're making sense. You can

have all that immediately.' Blue's eyes narrowed. 'As soon as I take possession of one thing.'

'Which is?'

'The Time and Space Machine.'

Harrison turned to Blue and knew he was about to seal his fate. His face softened for the first time since he'd arrived at Blue's castle. 'For you to even ask that, Theodoran, only confirms your complete lack of understanding of me or any of the principles Spy Force stands for.'

Blue's expression froze as if he'd been hit by a sudden ice storm. His mouth twisted into an ugly sneer of hate.

'Take him to the Portal Room.'

Kronch sprang forward as if he had been waiting for this very moment. He pinioned Harrison's arms behind him, wringing them between his sausage fingers into a painful twisting burn.

Blue seethed as he watched the head of Spy Force being led away. 'You have crossed me for the last time, Reginald Harrison. Let's see how clever you are now.'

CHAPTER 15

A SCOTTISH LANDING AND THE CRIES OF A DERANGED MADMAN

Max, Linden, and Toby appeared in a flash of fluorescent light and falling sparks of colour. They hung in the air for a few seconds before floating gently to a rocky cliff-top at the bottom of the hill leading to Blue's castle.

'That was insane!' Toby cried. 'What *was* that we just did?'

Max and Linden began searching for the stunted tree that hid the transported sack of Spy Force gadgets Dretch had told them about.

'We've just travelled at hyper-speed from Australia to Scotland using a Time and Space Machine,' Linden said a little smugly.

'Well, that's something I wasn't planning on doing today.' Toby looked up towards the castle. 'This Blue guy lives here? Tell me, is he a little man who spends most of his time making plans to dominate the world?'

Max looked up from her search. 'Pretty much.'

'Thought so.'

Linden's irritation towards Toby wasn't going away. 'It'd be great if you could help us find the pack instead of standing there talking.'

'No problem.' Toby frowned, unsure of where Linden's attitude was coming from. 'What's in this pack anyway?'

'Impact Suits, Undetectatrons, Danger Meters and hopefully a few other things that will make what we're about to do a little easier,' Linden explained.

'Excellent.' Toby had no idea what Linden had just said but it sounded like fun.

The wind swirled around them, buffeted up from the icy waters of the ocean below. The three searched the ground around the tree, poking into clumps of ragged, grassy scrub until Toby came across a small cloth bag. 'Is this it?'

'Hand it over.' Linden looked inside and smiled. 'Yep. Now put this on.' He handed over the Undetectatron. 'It keeps you hidden from all security devices. Just peel off the label and stick it to your chest.'

Toby took the Undetectatron and, lifting his jumper, did as he was told.

'And this Impact Suit will save you from any falls or knocks. It's like a suit of armour, a bullet-proof vest, and an airbag all in one,' Linden instructed. 'It goes over your underwear but under your clothes.'

'But I'll have to show off my muscly body.' Toby smiled at Max but realized she hadn't heard. She stood, barely moving, staring at the castle on the hill.

'Just put it on,' Linden whispered sternly as he handed Toby his last device. 'And this is a Danger Meter. At the slightest hint of danger you will feel a vibrating rhythm against your chest.'

Linden took off his pack and put the sack and its remaining gadgets inside. He quickly sent a message to Dretch telling him they'd arrived, but when he looked up, he noticed Max was still staring fearfully at the castle, turning the digital camera ring on her finger. He walked over to her. 'We're ready to complete our mission, boss.'

Max kept staring into the biting wind.

'We're going to find your mum and Harrison, Max. You know that, don't you?'

Max turned to him. 'Can we say the pact?'

'Of course,' Linden answered gently.

'What's the pact?' Toby called.

Max turned and saw a half-naked Toby stepping into his suit. Linden glared at him. 'Nothing you need to know about.'

'I think we should all say it,' Max whispered, turning away.

Linden held Max's hand and, after waiting for Toby to finish dressing, reluctantly offered his other hand to him. Max closed her eyes and began the pact, reciting word for word her promise to look after her two fellow spies. Linden repeated the promise, followed by Toby.

'Excellent,' Toby exclaimed. 'What do we do next?'

Linden walked over to his pack and took out his palm computer. He studied Dretch's map of the area and discovered a scrubby forest path that would take them directly to the castle. 'Follow me.' He'd never worried about it before, but suddenly he wanted to show that he was in charge. 'Now remember, Toby, Max and I have done this kind of thing lots of times, so all you need to do is follow us and not attract attention to yourself.'

But as Linden finished speaking his foot slipped on the muddy path and he flipped into the air, landing with a squelching bellyflop on a mound of damp moss.

'Sure thing, boss.' Toby smirked and offered to help him up.

Linden ignored him and, unearthing his hands from the mud, picked himself up. He winced, not from the fall, since the Impact Suit had kept him safe, but from making a fool of himself in front of Toby. He casually flicked off some mud from his arms and chin and led the way to the side of the castle and the gloomy edge of the moat.

He looked again at his palm computer. 'Dretch has marked an entry point on the top level of the castle.' He pointed upwards. 'It's through that archway and into an open-roofed courtyard.'

'How are we going to get there?' Toby frowned.

Linden slipped his computer into his pocket and pulled out the lever on his pack. 'We're going to fly. You'll have to come with me.'

'Fly? Of course. Why didn't I think of that?' Toby beamed.

'Actually, it'd be better if he came with me,' Max suggested. 'I'm lighter than you and the packs are going to struggle enough to lift our weight in this wind.'

'I'm not sure that . . .' Linden began, but Toby had already moved behind Max and put his hands around her. Linden felt a curious urge to pull him off and throw him to the ground.

Within seconds the three spies were in the air, navigating their way through the surging bursts of wind. Max gritted her teeth. There was a time when she had been hopeless at operating her Personal Flying Device, but after months of practice, she felt she had mastered it.

What she hadn't mastered, however, was her fear of heights. As they rose above the pitch black moat, Max looked down and her fear hit her like another gust of wind.

'Oh!'

Toby and Max tipped sideways along with her confidence.

Linden saw her faltering and guessed the reason, but just as he was about to warn Max not to look down, Toby got in first. 'You can't fly this thing any better?'

'I'm trying.' Max's voice was verging on panic.

'Maybe you should have taken a few lessons before you decided to risk my life.'

Max was annoyed that she was trying to save their lives and all Toby could do was criticize. 'And maybe you should just be quiet and let me fly this thing.'

'I would if you were any good at it.'

That was it. Max was furious. She gripped the lever of the flying pack even tighter. 'I'm one of the best spies Spy Force has. And one of the youngest!' The PFD sailed straight upwards as Linden looked on, navigating his own way through the wind. 'I've flown one of these through the middle of a volcano and . . .' Max headed towards the stone archway, 'saved one of Spy Force's top agents doing it.' She started taking the PFD in for a landing.

'And another thing . . .' But as they were about to land, a blast of frosty air rounded a stony corner of the castle, pushing them off-balance. The two hit the stone floor with a pounding thud and rolled to a bumpy stop metres from where they first touched down.

Linden saw the jostled landing. 'Max!' But she couldn't hear him over the wind.

'OK, you can get off me now!' Max wheezed as Toby's body was sprawled over hers.

Linden landed just behind them and raced over to Max. 'Are you OK?'

'Is she OK?' Toby cried getting to his feet. 'She's amazing! At school she never gets picked for any of the sports teams and here she is with this action-packed life that's better than most DVDs. Oh, and sorry for the dig about needing flying lessons.'

It was only then that Max realized what Toby had done. He'd picked a fight with her so she'd forget about her fear of heights.

'Very clever,' she smiled.

'Thank you.' Toby looked very pleased with himself.

Linden was confused. From the air it had looked as if they were arguing, but now they were all smiles. 'You were lucky you had your Impact Suits on.'

Linden was right. Toby only just now realized that after such a rough landing, he didn't hurt at all. 'I have got to get one of these.'

Linden was looking at his palm computer for their next move when he felt his Danger Meter vibrate against his chest.

'Anyone else feel that?'

No one had the chance to answer before two large hands moved out of the shadows and dug firmly into Linden's shoulders. He turned to see the outlines of three goons standing behind him.

'This isn't part of the plan, is it?' Toby's Danger Meter pounded against his chest as he too was taken captive.

Max shook her head despondently as Linden looked up at the towering men. 'Would you believe we got lost and were meant to be somewhere in Switzerland?'

The goons sniggered and grabbed all three, shoving them forward with their arms pinioned behind their backs.

'Take it easy! I'd like to use those arms again someday if that's OK,' Toby ordered, but his arms were pulled back even tighter. 'Thanks. That's much better,' he said sarcastically.

They were forced into a long circular stairwell that twisted its stony way deep into the castle's lower layers.

'How did they know we were here?' Max whispered to Linden. 'We have the Undetectatrons.'

'Maybe Toby didn't put his on quick enough.' There was a hint of blame in Linden's voice as he glared at Toby.

But Max thought it was something else. 'Or maybe they knew we were coming.' It was as if the goons had been waiting for them—but the only person who knew they were coming was Dretch. Max's heart jolted. Maybe instead of helping them, he was simply leading them to their deaths.

At the end of an increasingly narrow corridor, they came to a scratched and scarred metal door. One of the goons pulled out a key from a piece of elastic attached to his belt and opened the imposing structure.

'Ah, welcome, dear children, I've been waiting for you.'

Max's and Linden's eyes bulged as they faced Ms Peckham. She was one of Blue's closest assistants and they hadn't seen her since they had been kidnapped in London and threatened with being lowered into a vat of green jelly.[*]

She was immaculately dressed in a finely pressed skirt suit, polished shoes, and hair tied back in a bun that was wound so neatly it looked fake.

'You've arrived just in time,' she said in a voice as smooth as a hotel manager's. 'It's wonderful how we can always trust you to be great Superspies. Why do we bother having henchmen at all when you managed to get yourselves here on your own?'

'To make you feel superior because they have the intelligence of small rocks.' Max was furious that they'd been caught so easily.

Ms Peckham laughed quietly into her white-gloved hands. She nodded at the goons, and within seconds they had roughly torn Max's and Linden's packs from their backs and given them to her. 'You won't be needing these any more.'

Max shot Linden a panicked look.

Peckham went through the packs until she found what she was looking for. 'Ah, there you are.' She held the Time and Space Machine before her. 'It's about time you came home.'

---

[*] See *Max Remy Spy Force: The Time and Space Machine*

'It's not yours. It's Ben and Eleanor's!' Max shouted.

The goons sniggered and pushed Max, Linden, and Toby after Ms Peckham as she walked down a long stony tunnel punctuated by a series of bolted metal doors. Max felt the floor waver beneath her as she realized the magnitude of what she'd just done. Harrison hadn't used the Time and Space Machine to get here to avoid it falling into Blue's hands, and now she had pretty well handed it to him.

'You will be kept in one of these rooms until Mr Blue has decided what to do with you.'

'And maybe we don't want to be kept in one of these rooms.' Toby was tired of this woman's bossiness.

'You should have thought of that before you trespassed on private property.'

Ms Peckham's smile rose slowly. 'Take them in.'

The goons grabbed Max, Toby, and Linden even harder and thrust them along the tunnel after Ms Peckham. As they approached the last door, they heard angry muffled cries.

'Do you hear that?' Toby whispered to Max. 'We're not about to be thrown into a den with some half-crazed loony, are we?'

'No. Of course not,' Linden said abruptly.

But with each step that took them closer to the angry locked-in cries, Linden worried Toby might be right, and that their attempts to save Harrison and Max's mum were going to end in a small cell in the furthest corner of Scotland at the hands of a deranged madman.

CHAPTER 16
A CONFESSION AND A DANGEROUS DISCOVERY

The goons opened a thick metal door with an echoing drone and Max, Linden, and Toby came face to face with the person behind the deranged cries.

'Mum!' Max stared at the wild-haired, make-up-smeared woman gripping the bars of an inner cell door in front of her.

She was still wearing her wedding dress, but instead of the perfect white designer creation, she was swathed in a torn, frayed, and muddy disaster.

The goons unlocked the cell door and shoved the three of them inside, slamming it shut behind them. Max's mother grabbed her daughter and squeezed her so tight it was hard for Max to breathe.

'Oh, my little girl. My baby! Is it really you? What are you doing here?'

Max had thought so much about saving her mum she had forgotten to think about how she would explain why she was there.

'Well, Mum, it's like this. You see . . .'

Max's mum turned to the goons with a fierce snarl in her voice. 'What have you two brain-dead sacks of stupid done? She's just a little girl. It's bad enough that you kidnap a completely innocent woman, but now you're kidnapping children too!

What kind of inhuman apes are you? Why don't you get real jobs? Something more suited to your intelligence, like gathering slime off the bottom of a sewer. Or how about—'

'Ah, Ms Beckinsdale? Usually it's best not to upset these guys.' Linden gawped at the way Max's mum got angry in exactly the same way Max did.

'I'll give them upset, I've only just begun. When I've finished with them—'

'I can see where your feistiness comes from,' Ms Peckham said to Max in a mocking tone. 'Trouble is, it's not going to help either of you.'

She turned away with a jaunty step. 'That's all for now. I need to let Mr Blue know he has guests. Oh, and if you even try to escape, it will be the last thing you ever do.'

The metal door pounded shut as their captors left, reverberating with a clanging sound for whole seconds after they had gone.

'Hmmmph!' her mum snorted before turning her attention to Max. 'Oh, my sweet baby girl! Are you OK? Have they hurt you?'

There was so much Max had to tell her mum that it all came out in a panicked, garbled rush. 'I'm fine but I was so worried about you and when you were kidnapped from the wedding we didn't know who did it and where you were or what we should do and all I could think about was that you had to come back because I couldn't stand the idea that you'd never be here any more and that I'd never see you . . .' Max took a breath and slowed down. 'I couldn't see any reason for doing anything without you.'

'It's OK, sweetie. We're together now and I'm sure it won't be long until the police find us. Then we can go home, have nice warm baths and forget this ever happened.'

'It's a little more complicated than that, Ms Beckinsdale,' Linden said sheepishly.

'No, you're right. We'll have to answer questions first, of course. The police need to do their job. But as long as I'm with my beautiful girl, it doesn't matter where I am.' She gave Max another firm hug and nuzzled her in the cheek.

Toby raised his eyebrows, wondering how Linden was going to explain his way out of this one.

'No, I mean there won't be any questions.'

'They are going to want to ask questions to find out why these hooligans kidnapped me. That's how it works.'

'Not in this case,' Toby mumbled to himself.

'Mum?' Max's nerves sent a trembling spasm

through her whole body. 'We've come to rescue you.'

Max's mother smiled. 'That's very sweet but I'm not sure you and your little friends will be able to do anything about these brutes. My guess is they are seasoned criminals and this isn't the first time they have done this.'

There was a prickly silence in the room until Linden spoke up. 'Um, you're right. It's not. Max and I have come up against them a few times before.'

Max's mother's face fell. 'I'm sorry?'

Max had been able to keep her Spy Force identity a secret from her mother since she'd been made an agent, but now she was finally going to have to admit it.

'Mum, Linden and I are spies. We're part of an intelligence agency called Spy Force, which is based in London. We used a Time and Space Machine to travel here from Sydney to save you and our boss, Harrison, who we think Blue is going to kill.'

There was another heavy silence.

'Now, Max, I know things have been pretty traumatic these last few days, but I think I'd know if you were a spy.'

Linden tried to help. 'It's true, Ms Beckinsdale.'

No one knew what to do, until Max's mother decided for them.

'Don't give me this "I'm a spy" talk. You're a little girl whose life should be spent at home studying and talking on the phone and going to parties with your friends, not caught up in a world of Peckhams, Blues, and . . .' She glared at Linden, 'boys with way too much imagination.'

Max's sadness over her mother's kidnapping was suddenly pushed aside by a big dose of being fed up. She'd come halfway around the world to save her mother, breaking Spy Force rules and risking her life, and all she was getting was one of her usual lectures.

'And what about your life? You don't think I ever have a problem with that?'

Max's mother gasped. 'That is not the same thing, young lady.'

'Stop calling me young lady. Do you have any idea how irritating that is?'

Linden knew he was about to see one of those mother–daughter showdowns Max had told him about.

'Even on the other side of the world you still treat me like a kid, yelling at me and telling me what to do in front of other people, when I am a spy who has saved the world from criminals like Blue who only want to destroy it. And you know what? I'm actually good at it! But I know you're not going to believe that because you think I mess up everything I do.'

Max's mum frowned. 'That's not true, sweetie.'

'It is! You're always telling me I'm clumsy and careless and don't take care of anything properly, but being in Spy Force has taught me I'm good at lots of things.'

Max's mum stared open-mouthed at her daughter. 'But, sweetie, I . . .'

'What's that?' Toby saw a red light flashing through Linden's jacket pocket.

He took out his palm computer. 'It's Dretch.'

'Who's Dretch?' Max's mother asked.

'He works with us at Spy Force,' Linden answered. 'And apart from Peckham and her goons, he's the only other person who knows we're here.'

Max's mother took a few moments to realize what this meant. 'So the police aren't on their way?'

'No, but Spy Force is better than any—'

'I've heard enough about Spy Force for now!' she snapped.

Max had had enough of her mother and grabbed Linden's computer. 'Dretch.' Her voice was cold. 'We've been captured. As if they somehow knew we were here . . .'

'Captured?' Dretch flinched. 'Are you all safe?'

He seemed genuinely worried, or as worried as Dretch could get.

'Yes. For now. But Peckham's got the Time and Space Machine.'

Dretch's eyes got even wider.

'You knew nothing about this?'

Toby and Linden stared at Max, realizing what she was accusing Dretch of.

'Nothing.' Dretch looked deflated. 'I'll work out a way to get it back. For now, Harrison is in danger and needs our help. Quimby has been studying the unusual area of activity in the castle and has discovered that it is a highly charged field called a Portal Room.'

'A Portal Room?' Linden asked. 'You mean a room with entrances to different realities?'

'So you are as clever as they say?' Dretch smirked. 'When acted upon in a certain way, the particles in the room change shape, offering a gateway into another realm.'

The computer was snatched from Max's hand.

'Hang on a minute there, Fetch, I'm Max's mother and I want to know why you haven't sent someone here to save us.'

Dretch groaned at the woman who'd invaded his screen while Max fumed about the way her mother was behaving.

'Mum, it's because we need to save Harrison as well as you and bringing in the police at this point would only complicate everything.' She took a breath to calm herself down. 'Can I have the computer back now?'

'Not until I get an assurance from this Fetch fellow that he will organize our rescue immediately.'

Max's mum had a hysterical edge in her voice that meant she was only going to get worse. 'Mum, we're here to do that.' Max gritted her teeth. 'And his name is Dretch.'

'Ms Beckinsdale?' It was Toby. 'I know this has been a terrible time for you but Spy Force really is the best spy agency in the world, with gadgets even the most well-equipped police force doesn't have. Believe me, they are far better to handle this rescue than anyone else.'

Linden smiled knowingly. Toby may have thought he was saving the day, but once Max's mother was on a roll, no one could stop her.

But then, the strangest thing happened. She calmed down.

'I think Max needs her computer back now, Ms Beckinsdale,' Toby added gently.

She handed back the computer to a stunned Max.

Dretch continued. 'The Portal Room is one step up from the Nightmare Vortex that you were sucked into during the Annual Spy Awards Night.[*] It's a world of constantly changing realities that Quimby believes, in the wrong hands, could be very dangerous.'

'Is this what Blue is planning to use on Harrison?' Linden asked.

Dretch paused. 'He already is.'

A cold disquiet settled on the room.

'This is what we received from Harrison's button camera only minutes ago.'

Toby and Linden gathered around Max, staring incredulously at what they saw on the computer screen. Through Harrison's hidden camera, they saw Blue sitting on an ornate sofa in a high-ceilinged, regal room. He was surrounded by intricate tapestries

[*] See *Max Remy Spy Force: The Nightmare Vortex*

and paintings, carved cabinets and tables, and a man in a golden suit was serving tea.

'You have one more chance to give me what I want.' Blue sipped his tea innocently. 'Otherwise you will force me to activate my latest and perhaps most exciting invention: the Portal Room. A place of alternative realities that can be called up by a simple flick of these controls.'

Blue took a small black switch from his pocket.

'You could be dangled from the tops of glaciers, or thrown out of a plane without a parachute, or left stranded on a rotting raft circled by ravenous sharks. Things can get very nasty.'

'It is a tempting exchange. My life for one small machine,' an unseen Harrison answered.

'Ah, I was hoping you would see it my way. After all, you've made one Time and Space Machine, you can make another.' Blue's smile was so wide it almost reached the edges of his face. 'So, what's your final word?'

They saw Harrison's hand put his teacup and saucer on the gold tray before him. 'You're wasting your time, Theodoran. I will never give you what you want.'

Blue gripped the handle of his cup firmly. 'Even after what I have told you?'

'I am not a man who can be bought. Not for any price.'

'Blue's serious about that room,' Linden whispered to Max.

'I know.' At that moment they were so proud of their boss, they knew they'd do everything they could to save him.

Blue flinched in fury as Harrison sat before him refusing to be swayed.

'Then you and your precious Spy Force will pay!' He stood up and threw the cup against the wall, sending a shattered mix of tea and crockery ricocheting from a hanging tapestry before it fell tinkling to the floor.

He held the switch in front of him and was about to press down hard when there was a knock at the door.

It was Peckham. She had a Cheshire Cat grin on her face as she walked over to Blue, whose back was turned to Harrison.

Peckham whispered in his ear and discreetly handed something to him. Blue took her offering and put it in his pocket. He then murmured something which brought an even greater smile to Peckham's lips.

'It will be done immediately.'

'She's given him the Time and Space Machine,' Max guessed fearfully.

As Peckham left the room, Blue turned to Harrison triumphantly. 'Shall we?'

He pressed down on the black switch and a giant image of a snow-covered mountain swirled into view in the middle of the room, like an oversized floating movie screen.

'What was that he just did?' Max's mother stared.

'He's activated the Portal Room,' Max answered.

'But I thought you were just . . .'

'Shhhh, Mum. We need to watch this.'

Blue shot Harrison a smug look. 'It's a pretty picture, isn't it? But I wonder what would happen if we were to step inside?'

Blue moved to a small marble stand in front of the picture and placed his hand on one half of a small metallic dome in the centre.

'All you need to do is place your hand on the other side of this dome to create the energy field strong enough to pull us in.'

The image on the computer shuddered as if Harrison was being pushed towards the stand. His hand was forcibly planted on the dome and the two halves were pushed together. When contact was made, a swirling energy field tore from the now complete dome towards the centre of the image. A twisting, tornado-like wind snagged at Blue's clothes and hair, pulling them towards the snow-covered mountain.

'Here we go!' Blue was jubilant.

It was then, with a frantic blur, that the screen went black.

'Harrison!' Max called just as Dretch's face appeared on the screen. 'We've got to find him. Do you know where they are?'

'The coordinates of the Portal Room are on your map.' Dretch paused. 'It'll be very dangerous. The chances of coming out alive are difficult to predict.'

'Well, it's lucky for us we're not going!' Max's mother cried.

Max shot her a frustrated scowl before turning back to Dretch. 'We're a bit stuck at the moment but we'll get there as soon as we can.'

Dretch's eyes were edged with pride. 'Anything else you need, I'll be here.'

He then disappeared and the screen went black.

'I hope you don't think you're going to this Portal Room, young lady.'

Max looked up the map of the castle on the computer. 'We can't stand by while Harrison is in danger.'

'But Fetch just told us it'll be very dangerous.'

'It's Dretch,' Max reminded her again. 'And we'll be fine.'

Max knew the situation they were in was unusual but she wished that, just this once, her mother would trust her.

Linden tried to reassure Max's mum. 'Max and I have a pact to look after each other on every mission.'

'A pact? A pact isn't going to save my daughter's life, young man. And you heard that woman! If we try to escape it'll be the last thing we ever do.'

'They say that kind of thing all the time,' Linden explained.

Max's mum fixed Linden with a bitterly cold look. 'I am trying to have a conversation with my daughter, if you don't mind.'

'Linden's right, Mum. They say things like that to scare us into doing what they want.' Max tried to stay calm. She turned to Linden. 'The Portal Room isn't far from here, we just need to figure a way—'

'How long have you been dealing with these sort of people?'

'Mum, now is not the time to talk about this.'

Max's mother threw her hands on her hips in a way that made Linden and Toby blink. It was exactly the way Max would have done it.

'I think now is exactly the time to talk about this. In fact, I've got all the time in the world to hear you try to explain what you've been up to, and I'm not moving until—'

'Ah, Ms Beckinsdale?' Toby said gently. 'Max and Linden really are experts at this. They're the only ones who can save us and we need to trust them.'

Max wasn't sure what it was about Toby, but he had this way of making her mother calm down.

Until the walls started closing in.

'What's happening now?' Max's mother demanded.

Two walls on opposite sides of the cell began scraping along the dusty floor towards them.

'Looks like Blue has already decided what he wants to do with us,' Toby guessed.

'What? We've got to get out of here!' Max's mother took great gulping breaths, trapped in a choking panic.

The grinding sound of the moving walls echoed around the shrinking stone room, warning of a complete and crushing death.

Max and Linden desperately tried to work out what to do next.

'Any ideas?' Max looked towards Linden.

'Not yet, but I'm working on it.'

'Well, work on it a little faster, young man!' Max's mother ran towards one of the approaching walls and tried to push it back.

'Mum, can you be quiet so we can think?'

'But if we don't do something now we're going to die!'

The scraping of the walls groaned around them like thunder.

Toby gasped as he felt a damp chill of dusty air. The stone walls nudged closer.

'What's going to happen now? Are we going to die?' Max's mother screamed.

But Max couldn't answer. She tried to keep her thoughts calm and steady. After telling her mother she was a top spy who'd come to rescue her, it now looked as though their lives were about to end in one slow but definitive squelch.

CHAPTER 17

A NARROW ESCAPE AND AN ALTERNATIVE REALITY

The cold, coarse surface of the cell walls moved closer and closer, threatening a crushing, pulverizing death within seconds.

'We're going to die!' Max's mother screamed again, holding her arms out in a futile attempt to stop them.

'We're not going to die!' Max shot back, wishing her mum would stop saying the word die. 'We're going to . . .' She dredged her brain for ideas, hoping to come up with something, but nothing came. That's when Toby spoke up.

'Max, stand beside me.'

'What?'

'Just do it.' Toby stood with his shoulders facing the two moving walls. 'And Linden, stand on the other side of me.' Linden wasn't happy following Toby's orders, but knew he had no choice.

The two agents stood on either side of Toby as the walls nudged against their shoulders.

'What are you doing? You're going to kill my baby!' Max's mother screamed in horror until she couldn't stand it any longer and shut her eyes.

Just as the walls should have crushed them into flattened lifeless versions of themselves, the groaning sound of moving stone quietened and the walls came to a stop.

Max's mother opened her eyes to see the three agents standing shoulder to shoulder in front of her. 'What happened?'

'I think we just spoiled Blue's plans to do away with us.' Toby's pleasure in having saved them was all over his beaming face.

'The Impact Suits,' Max remembered with a smile.

'Yep. They're as good as you said they'd be, Linden.'

'You're amazing!' Max's mother was only just coming to terms with their escape from death. 'You really are one incredible boy, do you know that?'

Max gave Toby a smile full of admiration.

'It was just an idea.' Toby blushed.

'An idea that saved our lives!' Max's mother cried. 'And as much as I think this whole business is too dangerous for you all, I want to thank you for looking after Max.'

'Looking after Max?' Max and Linden cried in unison.

'I don't need looking after.' Max tried to throw her hands on her hips but they were jammed tightly against her sides.

'From what I've learnt today, I think you do! And another thing . . .'

'Mum, could we save the lecture for later? We have to get out of here and rescue Harrison.'

'And how exactly are we going to get out of here, young lady?'

Max let the 'young lady' comment slide and held out her finger with a triumphant smile. 'With this. It's a digital laser ring that will cut a hole in the wall and get us out of here. We just have to work out the best place to do it.'

'That'll be easy.' Toby beamed even more. 'Ms Beckinsdale, would you mind looking in my left sock?'

Max's mother bent down warily, lifted the leg of Toby's Impact Suit and pulled the X-ray Spectrogram out of his sock.

Linden frowned. 'Where'd you get that?'

'From your pack just after we landed. You were being a pain, acting all leaderly and bossy, so I thought I'd get you back.'

'Get me back?' Linden fumed. 'I was trying to help you—'

'We don't have time to argue, young man,' Max's mother instructed. 'Especially if Toby has something that will get us out of this squished prison. Go on, dear.'

'Actually, Linden is better at this than me.' Toby smiled modestly.

'I hope so.' Max's mother handed Linden the Spectrogram.

Linden was fuming but knew he couldn't say anything more. Toby's thieving may well help them find Harrison.

Although Linden's arms were pinned between the wall and Toby, he could just move his hands far enough to activate the device. He soon found a section of the wall that would lead them away from Peckham and straight towards the Portal Room.

Max held her ring at the exact spot and within minutes the laser had cut a hole through the stone wall.

'Mum, you go through first.'

Max's mother started to protest but reconsidered at Toby's reassuring smile.

'The rest of us are going to have to follow fast,' Max continued. 'Because as soon as one of us moves, the walls will start coming in again. When I count to three, we'll all turn sideways and run for it.'

Max counted and all three turned and dived through the hole as the sound of the closing walls started up again. On the other side of the cell was a cathedral-sized room, with tall ceilings and towering stained-glass windows.

'Where to now?' Max's mother was almost starting to enjoy herself.

Linden exchanged the Spectrogram for his palm computer and looked at the map. 'Follow me.'

Although Peckham would now think they were dead so no one would be looking for them, they still moved carefully through the winding corridors, ballrooms, and spiralling staircases of the castle, until they reached an imposing set of doors.

'This is it.' Linden used both hands to turn a large iron ring and an echoing click told them the doors were unlocked, but when they entered, what they saw before them left them chilled.

It was the regal room that Harrison's button camera had shown. The giant image of the snow-covered mountain still stood in the centre. Only now Harrison and Blue were *inside* the image, standing opposite each other, with the fury of a storm thrashing around them.

'The Portal Room is filled with many gateways to astounding places,' Blue was yelling with pride to Harrison. 'And this, I think, has to be one of my favourites.'

Max's heart was wrenched with fear. Harrison was a brilliant leader, but when it came to anything physical he was the clumsiest man she'd ever met.

She moved closer and reached out towards the image.

'Max, come back here,' her mother ordered.

It felt as if Max was touching a warm window made of gel. She pushed harder, but couldn't break through.

Inside the image, Blue held up a commanding hand and instantly a giant bird rose from below the cliff. Its wings fanned out around it like a giant sail, dwarfing the small body of Harrison.

'It's a golden eagle,' Toby said, staring in awe at the hovering bird of prey. 'They are one of the largest birds of prey and can kill by a single blow with their clawed feet.'

The bird swooped at Harrison, who ducked and fell to the snowy ground with a clumsy thud. The eagle turned and swooped again. Harrison tried to roll out of its way but was struck by the bird's powerful beak, which carved a deep gash in his face and sent him rolling towards the edge of the cliff.

'Mr Harrison!' Max called, watching the Portal Room's thick jellied wall as the bird turned with an ear-ringing squawk and dived to deliver another attack.

'Quick, Linden. Over here.' Max rushed to the marble stand.

'Maxine, come back here!' her mother called.

But Max wasn't listening. The giant image of Blue laughed above her and the eagle swooped, thumping into Harrison with its powerful foot.

'He's going to die!' Max cried as her chief tumbled over the edge, his hand reaching out just in time to grab onto a spindly tree.

Blue raised his hand as a signal for the bird to fly away. It veered off towards the darkened horizon. Its giant wingspan turned easily in the gusty winds as it began to spiral slowly downwards below the cliff, leaving its battered prey clinging for life at the edge of the rocky mountainside.

Max and Linden put their hands on the dome of the marble stand and instantly felt the stirrings of a powerful force swirl around them.

'There is no way you're going in there, Maxine,' her mother warned.

Harrison panted. His cheek was a bloodied mess but, just as he seemed done for, he used the tree to drag his battered body up and over the edge.

'Well, let's see what we have next,' Blue said teasingly as he held out the Portal Room switch.

The snowy surroundings began to spin around them.

Max's heart belted against her chest as the

force pouring out of the dome began to ruffle their clothes and hair. 'Can't this machine go any faster?'

'Max?' Toby called. 'Do you want me to come too?'

'No one's going anywhere!' Max's mother became increasingly hysterical.

'Linden and I can handle it,' Max answered Toby. 'It's going to be dangerous in there and we've been trained for these kind of situations.'

'You have? When?' her mother screeched.

'Can you stay and keep things calm here?' Max asked Toby.

Toby's shoulders sank a little. 'No problem.'

'Thanks.' Max smiled.

The force of the energy from the dome increased. Max and Linden felt themselves being drawn into the scene above them, which had finally settled so that Harrison and Blue found themselves on either side of an ocean-drenched blowhole.

'Max! You are not going in there and that's final.'

Max shot Toby a quick glance and he immediately came to the rescue.

'Ms Beckinsdale, you've been so great taking all this in. We've come so far to save you and Mr

Harrison, but if Max and Linden don't go now he may die.'

Toby was good but even he couldn't calm Max's mother down this time.

She strode over to her daughter and pulled her away from the marble stand, which instantly cut off the energy field. She held Max by the shoulders and looked her in the eyes. 'Now you listen here. Whatever this thing is above us is way too dangerous a place for a young girl and I refuse to allow any daughter of mine to even go near . . .'

As her mother's ravings continued, Max knew time was running out for Harrison and she had to do something to stop her mother from interfering. She turned to Linden. 'Have you still got that Knock Out Spray?'

Linden quickly handed over the spray. Max pointed it at her lecturing mother and pressed hard. Within seconds, she'd stopped yelling and had collapsed into the carefully placed arms of Toby, who lowered her gently to the floor.

'It'll be better this way,' he smiled. 'Just make that rescue quick, eh?'

Max put the spray in her pocket, raced back to the stand and replaced her hand on the dome.

'Max.' Toby had one last thing to say. 'Be careful.'

Max smiled as the suctioning force again began to swirl around them until it was tugging at their bodies and pulling them towards the virtual world above. A world that held the frail and injured Chief of Spy Force.

'Let's get him, eh?' Linden saw the look of worry on Max's face and gave her a wink. He knew what she was thinking. They were good spies, but what they were about to face would test every ounce of their courage and skill. There was only one thing standing between them and Harrison's rescue, and it was the one man who wanted him dead.

The suctioning pull reached its peak and in one jet-fast sweep, they were flung into the centre of the alternative reality of the Portal Room.

CHAPTER 18
THE PORTAL ROOM

'Oomph!' Max and Linden landed with a painful thud behind a large rock as a wild ocean swelled restlessly around them.

A few metres away, Harrison and Blue stood on either side of the rocky fracture of the blowhole. It exploded with a volcanic surge of water, raining a spray of freezing drops all around them.

Blue threw Harrison a laser gun. 'I don't want the fight to be unfair. Though you were never any match for me when we worked together as agents.'

Blue pointed his laser at Harrison and sent a burning red beam pounding into his chest. The Impact Suit stopped the beam from cutting into his body, but the force of the laser sent him thumping to the ground. Blue frowned, knowing the laser should have done much more damage than a mere push.

Max wanted to run to Harrison's aid, but Linden held her back. 'If Blue sees you now, he'll kill you.'

'You were once a superb agent, Theodoran, we both know that,' Harrison gasped. 'But your ego got in the way and ruined your sense of perspective.'

Blue seethed, flinging his arms into the air. 'Perspective?' The whites of his eyes grew brighter as another burst of water surged through the blowhole. 'I'll give you perspective. I was Spy Force's most loyal and hard-working agent. I gave my life to that agency for years, trying to gain your recognition, trying to get you just once to say I was doing a good job.'

Max watched as Harrison again dragged himself up. His cheek was still bleeding and his suit was torn, with a burnt hole across his chest. The sight of him sent an ache through Max's heart. She held out her laser ring and tried to get a fix on Blue's gun.

'It's a shame that your need for recognition became bigger than your need to do good.' In a trigger-fast move, Harrison held his laser out and delivered a marksman-like blow to Blue's hand. The laser sprang from Blue's grasp, bouncing across the rocky platform before it plunged into the yawning mouth of the blowhole.

'Go, Harrison!' Max whispered.

'You've improved since we last met,' Blue reluctantly conceded. 'But this time we're not parting until this is done.'

'Done?' Harrison saw a crooked smile crawl onto Blue's lips.

'Until one of us is dead.'

Max's fear rose in her like a wave of nausea.

'That's it.' She again took aim. 'I'm going to strike him in the leg just badly enough to let us get Harrison out of here.'

She held the ring firm, determined to hit her mark, but when Max tried to activate it, nothing happened. That's when she looked at it closely and saw that the face was cracked. 'It's broken,' she breathed.

Linden thought quickly. 'The Knock Out Spray. If we can get close enough to Blue we can use that. Follow me.'

The wind swirled around them like a ghostly warning as they slowly crept behind large rocks and into darkened crevices out of Blue's line of sight.

Harrison held Blue's gaze, not wanting to flinch for a second at his challenge. 'Why don't you just get on with whatever retaliation you have in mind?'

Blue lunged forward. 'Always the smart one, aren't you, Harrison? You've always thought you were so much better than me. Better than everyone. Well, you're not!'

Another burst of water showered into the air, exploding over their heads.

'Look at your record as leader.' Blue shouted into the wind as Max and Linden crept into position behind him. 'In the last year Spy Force has come up against some of its most fabulous security breaches and bungles. Agents have been kidnapped while others have almost lost their lives in my Nightmare Vortex. Expensive vehicles have been destroyed in waterfalls and crash landings and the entire agency was at the mercy of a potentially fatal sleeping sickness, sneaked in by one of your own agents.'

'Under your control!' Harrison winced, not only at having reacted to Blue's taunts but because he had just spied the anxious faces of Max and Linden.

'He's seen us,' Max whispered.

Harrison continued as if he'd seen nothing. 'I trust every Spy Force agent with my life. You never have nor ever will know anything of loyalty or even the smell of it.'

'You and your loyalty! Well, if your agents are so loyal, how come I have this?'

Blue held up the Time and Space Machine.

Max looked on guiltily.

'Yes, your precious Time and Space Machine! Your agents are so loyal they gave it to me.'

Harrison didn't flinch. He was used to Blue's sad and pathetic lies and knew that none of his agents would have willingly given Spy Force's most valuable invention to their enemy.

'I am twice the scientist you will ever be,' Blue crowed. 'Look at the Doppelgänger! The world has been messing about with cloning for years and I've invented a device that does the same thing without all the fuss and expense. And now I have the Time and Space Machine as well, I suspect I will become very rich and very respected. I may even be given a Nobel Peace Prize!'

'You were kicked off the Force for agreeing to sell the plans for those two devices. Have you learnt nothing from your dismissal?'

Blue smiled broadly. 'I'll remember that when I collect my prize.'

'I'm not sure you will be getting any prizes for peace when the world finds out you faked your own death and stole the plans and devices from Spy Force.'

Blue's sizzling rage was barely concealed behind his puce face and twitching brow. He was done with talking. He had what he wanted, and it was time to complete what he'd come here to do.

Max and Linden were almost close enough to use the Knock Out Spray when Linden saw Blue pocket the Time and Space Machine and pull out a small disc. Blue then flicked a switch which sent a stream of sparks pouring from it.

'It's electrified.' Linden shuddered.

In one smooth action, Blue hurled it towards Harrison. It sizzled through the air in an electric blaze just as Linden flung a large rock into its path. The rock struck the disc, sending it off course, but not far enough. The disc left a burning gash in Harrison's unprotected hand.

Harrison stumbled to his knees just centimetres from the watery chasm of the blowhole, the pain searing through his hand like a burning whip.

Blue spun round, searching for what had thwarted his attack.

He then saw Max and Linden and his eyes bulged in anger.

'You were supposed to be crushed by the walls of the Pulverizing Cell,' he yelled, then calmed down and smiled. 'At least this gives me a chance to thank you personally for bringing me the Time and Space Machine, Maxine. I knew if I made you mad enough you would deliver it straight into my hands. And now, not only will Harrison die but I'll have the pleasure of personally killing you two as well.'

Blue reached into his pocket and took out a

grenade. 'This may not be one of my creations but it certainly is effective.'

'Run!' Max yelled at Linden as Blue threw the bomb. It exploded behind them in a blast of smoke and flying debris just as they jumped into a dark and rocky crevice. They ducked and covered their heads with their arms to shelter from the pelting shower of sharp rocks.

'Lie still,' Max instructed Linden as the dust from the explosion settled. 'Let him think we've been hit.'

The Impact Suits had saved them from the brunt of the blast, but they had not been able to stop a jagged piece of rock striking Max's forehead.

Blue looked through the clearing bomb smoke and walked over to see the two spies lying still, covered with a jagged spray of rubble. Confident that they were dead, he turned to Harrison and reached into his jacket pocket for his final weapon.

'I've had enough of playing.'

Max and Linden sneaked to the top of the crevice and saw him take out a black leather glove, his face plastered with a sickening smirk.

Harrison lifted his head and stared desolately at the place where Linden and Max had fallen. 'You may kill me but you will never destroy Spy Force.'

Blue said nothing, only smiled as he knelt down beside him.

'This little creation is a Heart Stopper. Its name says it all. Shall I give you a demonstration?'

Blue pressed his gloved hand hard onto Harrison's chest above his heart. Harrison sucked in an immediate coarse and wheezing breath as the glove lit up like a neon blue skeleton.

Max and Linden stared in horror. The protection of the Impact Suit seemed unable to repel the power of the Heart Stopper. The Spy Force chief gasped small breaths as his remaining strength was drained from his body.

Blue smiled through clenched teeth, enjoying the final struggling seconds of Harrison's life.

'I have waited a very long time for this moment, Reginald.'

Linden studied the glove. 'There seems to be a power source at the wrist which is sending currents of electricity along each finger. If we can break that connection we should be able to stop it.'

'But how?' Then, as Max asked the question, she saw it. The crackling electrified disc Blue had struck Harrison with earlier. 'I think we've just found out.'

Max scrambled quickly out of the crevice and

crawled over to the disc. She pulled the sleeve of her Impact Suit down over her hand and picked it up, smiling as she felt none of the electric current spitting from it.

She turned to Linden, who gave her a nod of encouragement. They both knew Max would have only one chance to hit the Heart Stopper. If she missed, not only Harrison's but Max's and Linden's fate would be sealed.

Max took careful aim and, taking a steadying breath, launched the disc into a sparkling path through the air and made a direct hit on the glove. Blue lurched backwards as the two power sources collided and the Heart Stopper exploded in a crackling fury of short-circuiting sparks.

Blue looked at the glove in fury and confusion as it sat useless and deactivated on his hand. He stood up and unbuckled it in anger, before tearing it off and throwing it behind him.

Seeing Blue off guard, Harrison lunged at him with a wrenching scream. The force of the impact caused Blue to hit the ground with a grunt of pain. The Time and Space Machine was flung from his pocket and landed on the rocks with a loud crack.

Max spied the fallen device. Desperate for it

not to be broken, she sprang forward and scooped it up as the two men gripped each other in an uncontrollable fury.

An incoming wave churned and thudded beneath them like a volcano threatening to erupt. Another explosion of water gushed up and fell in a drenching wall over Blue and Harrison. The sucking rush of the sea back into the blowhole dragged them closer to its edge. The two men then rolled to a precarious stop. Blue gave a frightened scream as he lay on his back, his head dangling over the edge of the blowhole, with Harrison's hands still gripping his collar.

'We can end this now, Theodoran,' Harrison offered. 'You can lose your life, or keep it and return to prison where you belong.'

Blue heaved great clawing breaths and again looked behind him to see the blackened chasm of raging sea beneath him.

'Yes. Yes, prison please!'

Linden moved beside Max. They both knew Blue could not be trusted, but also knew that for Harrison to kill a man went against everything he believed in.

Harrison eased his grip, slowly stood up and offered his hand.

Blue accepted the offer, stood before him and smiled. 'Sucker!'

He kicked Harrison's legs out from under him, forcing him to the slippery ground facing into the blowhole. Blue then pounced on Harrison and the two men wrestled even closer to the edge.

'He needs our help,' Max cried, but as they leapt forward, another volcano-like explosion of sea water drenched the air around them in a torrential downpour. This time the wash of water back into the blowhole took both men with it.

'Harrison!'

Max lunged towards the blowhole and fell to her knees, desperately trying to see a sign of her boss, but when she looked down, there was just a black, churning chasm.

'Max!' Linden ran forward and knelt beside her, desperate to get her away from the edge before another wave crashed over them. 'Come on.'

But Max couldn't move, her grief cementing her to the smooth ocean-washed ground. Little rivulets of water trickled along the stony platform before falling over the edge into the blowhole. She felt herself falling forward, drawn by the churning pull of the ocean and her anguish at having witnessed Harrison's fall.

'Let's go, Max.' Linden held her shoulders and carefully lifted Max to her feet, moving her away from the watery chasm. When they were far enough away, she collapsed to the ground.

'I tried to save him,' she yelled over the noise of the sea. Her devastation was so great it felt as if she was the one who'd been thrown into the surging ocean waters.

'I know.' Linden's throat ached at his held-back tears.

'I tried so hard but it wasn't enough.' Her anguish wrenched Linden's heart, tearing into him as he tried to comfort her.

'Linden.' She looked up at him with desperate eyes. 'What are we going to do?'

Linden didn't know. They had the Time and Space Machine and Max was safe, but apart from that, he did the only thing he could. He pulled Max in close and hugged her tight and they both cried knowing that Harrison, their beloved Spy Force leader, was dead.

CHAPTER 19
A SAD HOMECOMING

'Where are we going?' Max dragged her feet as a white-coated orderly led the way down the highly polished corridor.

'My orders were to come and get you. Beyond that I can't say a thing.'

'My mother's OK, isn't she?'

'She's fine.'

Max, Linden, and Toby were back at Spy Force. Toby had entered the Portal Room soon after Blue and Harrison's fall to warn them that his Danger Meter was going crazy and that they had better leave in case Blue's goons were on their way. Despite their grief, Max and Linden had left the Room and, hoping the damaged Time and Space Machine would still work, used it to transport all four of them back to London HQ.

Max's mother was immediately taken to the infirmary. She was diagnosed as fine and the effects of the Knock Out Spray kept her sleeping soundly.

Max followed the medical assistant in a daze. Her gashed forehead had been cleaned and bandaged and the dull, painful throb it left behind created a rhythm for her heavy footsteps. Even though they were safe within the protected walls of the Force, the battle at Cape Wrath had left an empty, black feeling in her chest and she felt more tired than she ever had.

Linden walked beside her, telling her some of his mum's most positive sayings, but even her best ones couldn't lift Max's mood.

'You were amazing back there, Max,' Toby said gently. 'I was watching the whole time. You did everything you could to save Harrison and I know he's proud of you, even now.'

'Thanks, Toby,' Max whispered so quietly they could barely hear her.

At the entrance to the infirmary the orderly left them in the presence of a large round nurse called Hilda, who began to bark a list of orders.

'I want you all to be quiet. This is a hospital, and unless you want to be mooshed into small spy pieces, you will act in a manner that is in accordance with the rules of the hospital, which are: one, you will at all times . . .'

'Just let them in, Hilda!'

Max's gaze flicked past the large nurse towards the gruff, wheezing voice coming from the nearest room. The look on Hilda's face told them she wasn't used to being spoken to like that, and that she also had no choice but to obey.

'Don't just stand around then, follow me,' she snapped.

They followed Hilda's stern step into the room, where they saw a cluster of white-coated staff hovering around the bed of an unexpected patient.

'Mr Harrison!' Max flung herself at the bandaged white figure in the hospital bed.

'How did you get here? Are you OK? I thought you were . . .'

Hilda pulled the over-excited girl off her patient and outlined his health. 'Mr Harrison has a mild case of exposure, a deep gash on his face, and a burn on his hand and chest. He's been given a natural stimulant and healing potion that will mend his wounds and strengthen his heart, after which, with complete bed rest, all will be fine.'

'Hilda, as much as I value your care, I'm still very much in control of my sense of hearing and would appreciate it if you would stop talking to people like I'm not here.'

Harrison hated being in the infirmary and was being fussed over by the same staff who had kept bothering him when the sleeping sickness had struck only a few months before and he had been one of its victims.[*]

[*] See *Max Remy Spy Force: The Amazon Experiment*

'But, Mr Harrison, sir, I was just—'

'Why don't I call you when I need you, Hilda? You've been wonderful, but I do need time to talk to my . . .' It was then Harrison noticed Toby. 'Agents?'

Hilda was obviously miffed and turned to leave. 'I'll be at my desk.'

Max stared at the man she'd only recently seen fall to a seemingly inescapable death. 'How did you survive, sir? We saw you fall.'

'About halfway into the blowhole, I luckily landed with a bit of a thud on a large ledge. Quimby made me take my super-grip gloves, which enabled me to pull myself to safety. I searched for you two but, realizing you were gone, I contacted Spy Force with the two-way radio on my jacket button. It was then Steinberger told me that not only you but also your mother had escaped and were safely back at Spy Force. I asked for the Invisible Jet to be sent but, as it happened, Dretch had already convinced Alex and Suave to fly to my rescue in it. I activated my Undetectatron, left the Portal Room and met them on an isolated part of the castle roof.' Harrison tried to look annoyed. 'Even though my orders were not to move until I gave the word.'

'But it's because of that you're still alive.' Max looked at her boss's grey wispy hair and bandaged cheek.

'Max, I am only one person. Spy Force will continue well beyond the day when I am no longer here.'

Max didn't want to think about that. 'You were incredible out there, sir. What you did was so brave. Your life was at stake and you never once gave in to Blue's demands.'

Harrison blushed and pretended to straighten out his sheet. 'You would have done the same thing.'

'Sir?' Linden asked. 'Is Blue really dead this time?'

'Yes he is.' There was a sad lilt to Harrison's voice. 'I know you will find this hard to understand, but Theodoran and I, I mean Blue and I, made a great team. He did once know the meaning of goodness, but it became lost to greed, and in the end, the anger he's held about being kicked out of Spy Force shrivelled any sense of fair play.'

Harrison looked down at his bandaged hand. 'I want to thank all three of you for your bravery and courage. Even though I've lost count of how many rules you broke.' Harrison flashed Toby a pointed look. 'You have become magnificent spies, with finely tuned instincts and a strong sense of what is right.' He sighed. 'But this also means that when you know what you think is right, Max Remy, you are no good at following orders.'

'Sorry, sir.' She offered a cheeky smile.

'You two are a good team.' A tear teased the corner of Harrison's eye. 'Always cherish that.'

Linden's beaming smile lit up beneath his crazed hair. 'I know.'

'They are a great team, Mr Harrison,' Toby burst in. 'You should see them in action. They're unbelievable. It's like watching some kind of stunt show.'

Max thought she could now try and explain Toby. 'Sir, I know we're not supposed to involve non-Spy Force personnel on our missions, but Toby was very good. He really helped out, especially when it came to dealing with my mother, which I've never seen anyone do before. He was very—'

'Max, you don't need to say any more.' Harrison paused. 'You do realize the Neuro Memory Atomizer is on its way here?'

'What's that?' Toby had a feeling it had something to do with him.

'Something that erases all memory of the

mission from your mind.' Max's disappointment was clear.

'So I won't remember any of it?' Toby asked.

Max nodded.

'There goes selling my story to the papers,' Toby joked. 'I was planning on being famous with this.'

'Actually, the Atomizer is for Max's mum. We think it best she remembers nothing of this. But Toby . . .' And here Harrison looked at Toby with a hint of a smile. 'From what I've heard, I think we may have found ourselves a new agent. After a few more checks and tests, of course.'

Toby's face lit up. 'Me? A new agent? That would be great, sir! Thank you, sir! That'd be excellent! I didn't mean it about selling my story to the papers, I promise . . .'

'Can I come in?'

Max turned. 'Steinberger!' She ran and threw herself at the Administration Manager, who did his best not to fall over.

'Welcome back, team!' He then saw Toby. 'Plus one. Your mission to bring back Harrison and Max's mother, although unauthorized, has been successful.' He gave Max a stern look. 'Mind you, if things hadn't gone so well you would have been in serious trouble.'

Max smiled, knowing Steinberger would find it hard to stay angry at them.

'And, Max, there's someone in the corridor who wants to talk to you.'

Max hesitated before walking outside. Standing there with his rumpled maroon coat and spaghetti hair was Dretch.

'I wanted to welcome you back,' he said.

'Thanks.' Max stood awkwardly beside him, embarrassed that after all he'd done, she had doubted him during the mission. 'I'm sorry for thinking you told Blue about us. It's just that . . .'

'You completed your mission. That's all that's important.'

There was another stilted silence. 'Better go,' Dretch mumbled and moved away.

'Dretch.'

He turned back. 'Mmm?'

Max walked forward and gave him a hug. 'Thank you,' she muffled into his coat.

The old man lifted his hands into the air and looked around. His face twisted into a confused scowl, until finally and slowly he lowered his arms and put them around her. 'You're welcome.'

Dretch then pulled himself away. He gave Max

a wrinkled smile and, putting his hands safely back in his pockets, walked away.

Max re-entered the hospital room just in time for Harrison's announcement.

'And Steinberger has some good news.'

The three agents looked at Steinberger. 'Alex and Suave have captured Sorenson. He was disguised as an old woman in a small deli in Luxembourg.'

'So all in all a very successful mission, I would say,' Harrison declared. 'But for now, it's time you went home. And, Toby . . . we'll be in touch.'

Steinberger held out the slightly scratched Time and Space Machine and called up Toby's details from when they had sent him home after the Hollywood Mission.

Toby turned to Max. 'I can't believe the same uptight girl I picked on at school turns out to be the most incredible person I've ever met.' He gave her one of his best smiles. 'I can't wait to do it all again. This is going to make moving to Europe a whole lot better.'

Max blushed and looked away.

'See you on the next mission, eh, Linden?'

Linden nodded, a small jealous ache in his chest.

When Harrison gave the nod, Steinberger pressed 'transport' on the Time and Space Machine, adding a brilliant green light to the room. A few seconds later, Toby was gone.

'Don't tell Hilda we did that in here or she'll moosh me into little bits.' Steinberger handed Max a small purple bottle. 'This is Wake Up Spray to use on your mother once you're at Ben and Eleanor's, who've offered to look after you until you've all rested. And since the media have camped outside your house in Sydney, we feel it's best for you to stay at Mindawarra until things settle down.'

'Your aunt and uncle have been very worried about you and can't wait to de-flea you,' Harrison said.

Max saw Harrison's disappointment at mixing up his words sink into him. 'I mean *see you.*'

'Sir? I know the word thing bothers you, but I think you're perfect the way you are.'

Harrison's smile was like standing in front of a cosy fire. 'Funny kind of perfect.'

'It's the best kind. And while you were facing Blue, you didn't stumble once.'

'Really?' Harrison settled into his pillow with a look of pride. 'Fancy that.'

Max then thought of something else. 'How's Quimby?'

'She's not very happy about her gadget count not matching up. You know how protective she is of her inventions. I told her you would make it up to her next time you saw her.'

Max's face fell. It was now she was going to have to say it. 'I'm not coming back, sir. I don't want to be a spy any more.'

Linden felt as if he'd been slammed against a wall. He thought after they'd completed their mission Max would forget about not wanting to be a spy.

Harrison shot a look at Steinberger, who gave a sad shrug. 'Let's talk about this when you've had time to rest and recover, Max.'

'I'm sure about my decision, sir. And besides, now you have Toby.' Max's voice cracked as she realized this might be the last time she would ever see him. And Steinberger, and Spy Force.

To stop herself from crying she threw herself into his blanketed chest. Harrison felt her body quiver in his arms. It was supposed to be the end of a mission, not the end of her career as a spy. 'Thank you for everything, Max Remy.'

Max pulled herself away. 'I'm ready to go now.'

Harrison flung off his covers, grabbed his dressing gown and stepped out of bed.

'Let's go to your mother's room and get you all home, eh?'

Although his body ached and he'd been confined to bed, he wasn't going to miss the chance to say farewell to one of his top spies for ever.

CHAPTER 20

A LAST GOODBYE

AND A

LONG-AWAITED DECLARATION

As Agent Max Remy guided the Invisible Jet into the Vehicular All-Response Tower at the world's most elite spy agency, it was as if she was entering a fictional place from a book. A creation of someone's imagination, not the place where she'd been a secret agent and gone on impossible missions to save the world from cruel and criminal minds.

Mr Blue, Spy Force's most vile archenemy, was gone, and with him went Max's desire to go on. She had once wanted the life of a spy as if everything she was depended on it, but now, for the first time since she'd joined Spy Force, she wanted to be a normal girl again.

She stepped out of the jet and headed towards the centre of the VART. Each step she took pinched at her, as if she was walking over glass. She stopped and looked around the vast hangar with its jets, oscillating motorbikes, and inflatable buggies. It was as much a home to her as her bedroom. And now she had to say goodbye.

She'd asked no one to come, it would be less painful that way. If she was going to cry, she didn't want it to be in front of the world's best spies.

She took the Time and Space Machine from her pocket and blinked away the tears that refused to stay put.

Footsteps clicked across the metal boardwalk behind her.

Max turned around.

'Alex!' It came out as a whisper.

'I couldn't let you leave without saying goodbye.'

Alex Crane, Spy Force's top agent, climbed down the stairs and walked over to Max. The two stood in front of each other, time weighing heavily between them.

'I thought you didn't like goodbyes.' Max knew about Alex's habit of disappearing as soon as a mission was completed.

Alex smiled. 'Max, I don't know many people who are big fans of goodbyes. And the thing is, as you get older, they don't get easier, but some of them are too important to stay away from.'

She moved closer to Max and put her arms around her. 'I hate seeing you go. You remind me of myself as a girl, and I wanted so much to see you grow into an even wiser and better spy.'

Max couldn't speak. She knew her decision to leave Spy Force was right, but why did it have to be so hard?

'We'll be here if you change your mind.'

Alex gave her one last hug and walked down the boardwalk of the VART.

Max held the Time and Space Machine and looked around for the last time.

'Goodbye, Spy Force.'

She pressed 'transport' and she was gone.

Max put the lid on her pen and closed her spy notebook. Its cover was torn and patched and its pages had dog-ears almost as big as Ralph's.

As if he knew he was being thought about, the great fluffy mutt looked up and whined. He'd made himself comfortable at Max's mum's feet and had been there ever since they'd arrived, as if he'd appointed himself her personal guardian. 'Don't worry, you're still my favourite dustbowl,' Max told him.

Max was in Ben and Eleanor's lounge room at Mindawarra. She looked at her mother as she slept on the sofa. Usually she was frantic, rushing from one celebrity and party to another, in a life that had very little to do with Max. She'd never been a fan of the country but as she lay asleep, wrapped in one of Eleanor's hand-woven blankets, she looked right at home.

Max smiled as she realized that with her tousled hair and no make-up, her mother looked prettier than Max had ever seen her.

It was then she opened her eyes. 'Have I been asleep long?'

'Not too long.' Max grinned cheekily before adding, 'Rip Van Winkle.'

'You loved that story as a kid, remember?' Max's mother shifted herself upright.

'I only made you read it every night for two years.'

'Was it only two?'

'Funny.' Max smirked. 'I hope you're hungry, because Ben and Eleanor are in the kitchen making enough food for everyone within a hundred kilometres.'

'I feel like I've been on a trek to the North Pole I'm so hungry.'

It had been explained to Max's mother that she'd been kidnapped by a criminal gang who saw her celebrity wedding as a way of making money from a ransom. The kidnappers had been captured, but had given Max's mum something that had knocked her out, so she wouldn't remember any of it.

She frowned. 'I keep having these strange dreams about being trapped somewhere gloomy and you coming to rescue me.'

'And did I?'

'Yes, you did.' Max's mum smiled. 'You were really quite brave.'

'Of course I was,' Max said proudly. 'Sorry about the wedding. I know how much you wanted it.'

'Well, I've been doing a lot of thinking about that, and I think maybe it's best if Aidan and I wait a while before we try to get married again.'

'Really?'

'Yes, really, and you could try not to look so excited about it.'

Max tried to look sincere. 'Sorry.'

'That's OK. I know it wasn't easy sometimes sharing a house with him.'

Max thought back on all the times she'd made her mum feel bad about Aidan and been mean to him. 'It wasn't that bad.'

Her mum's eyebrows snapped upwards.

'OK, sometimes it was. Especially that smell. He did use a lot of aftershave.'

Her mother laughed. It sounded light and breezy, and Max thought how nice it was to hear. 'He offered to come down to Mindawarra, but I wanted just to be with you and the family.'

Max smiled. This was the first time she'd heard her mother call Ben and Eleanor family.

'Max, this whole thing has made me realize that I've let things like my work and the wedding take over my life, and that I haven't been paying enough attention to you.' Her eyes filled with sadness. 'The thought of losing you frightens me more than anything.'

Max's heart felt as if it tripped over itself. It was true her mother always seemed too busy for her, but it was because of Max's spy work that they had almost lost each other. She wanted to tell her mum how it had felt when she thought she was dead, how she had felt somewhere inside her that she'd died too. But their mission had to be a secret and she couldn't say any of it.

'That's handy because I've got used to you being my mum, so I guess that means we're stuck with each other.'

Max's mum laughed, but at the edge of her vision, Max saw something that made her face fall into a bad-tempered scowl. 'No you don't!'

She spun round to face Geraldine, her number one archenemy chicken. 'I know why you're here and you're not going to get away with it.'

'I just wanted to see how you both were.' Eleanor stood at the door holding a steaming tray of vegetarian pasties, quiches, and pies.

'Sorry, Eleanor, not you. Her.'

'The chicken?' Max's mother asked, confused.

'She's not *just* a chicken. She's always after me.

She was probably about to dump flour on my head or eat my jumper or leave a giant poo right where I was about to sit.'

'But you're sitting already.' Linden poked his head in behind Eleanor, carrying another tray full of spring rolls, salads, and fresh, crusty bread.

'You think that makes any difference to her?'

'What's going on in here then?' Ben put down his tray of cheeses, biscuits, and homemade dips and chutneys, before reaching into his pocket for a tube of ointment. He starting applying it to Geraldine's foot. 'Now just a small squirt of this and we'll have you back to the yard in no time.'

Max was sceptical. 'She has a sore foot?'

'She snagged it on some barbed wire. Poor thing, must have really hurt.'

Ben gently picked up the chicken and placed it in a basket near Max. 'A night sleeping in luxury ought to fix it.'

Eleanor and Linden found themselves seats as Geraldine gave Max a happy cluck, but Max needed a lot more convincing before she would believe the chicken's kamikaze days were over.

'Hello?' A voice called from outside.

'It's about time you turned up.' Ben got up and made his way to the front door.

Moments later, he re-entered the room with his arm around the shoulders of a tall, wild-haired man with an oversized woollen jumper and patches in both knees of his jeans.

'Just in time. We've brought the food out. Mind you, there's more in the oven.'

Eleanor tugged Ben aside and gave the visitor a hug. 'Come in, Harry. It's good to see you.'

Max whispered to Linden. 'Who's he?'

'My dad,' Linden answered, biting into a roll.

'Your dad?' It was then Max realized he did look like a taller, older version of Linden. He had the same hair, same smile, and same relaxed way of standing.

'Let me do the introductions,' Eleanor began. 'This is my sister, Anna.'

'Hi.' Linden's dad suddenly looked as if he didn't know what to do with any part of himself.

'Hello.' Max's mum, who'd normally take over a conversation at this point, said nothing more.

'And this is the wonderful Max.'

Linden's dad walked over and shook her hand. He had soft skin and gentle, smiling eyes. 'I feel like we've already met.' He gazed at her a little longer. 'And you're just as pretty as Linden said.'

Ben slapped him on the back. 'She is, isn't she?'

'We think so,' Eleanor added.

Max blushed as the whole room focused on her for what seemed like hours.

'It's true,' Max's mum added with quiet pride.

Now Max felt really awkward and hoped someone would say something to shift the attention from her. Ben's stomach finally came to the rescue. 'Time to eat, I reckon. Linden, you sit with Max and make room for your dad.'

Plates, forks, and knives were handed around, along with the trays packed with food. Ben immediately launched into one of his many stories about when they were younger. Eleanor and Max's mum kept interrupting when they felt he got carried away and was exaggerating, but mostly they just laughed and wanted to hear more.

Max and Linden listened as they ploughed through their food, giggling at Ben's overacting and the way he held off the end of the story for ages, savouring every minute of the limelight.

When Max was full, she turned to Linden and whispered, 'It's your dad.'

'Yeah. I know.' Linden smirked. 'I recognized him.'

Max frowned. 'I mean . . . I just never thought I'd meet him.'

Linden and Max were squashed on a big sofa away from the adults. 'He hasn't been very social since Mum died. This is the first time he's stayed when there have been strangers here. I think your mum is the reason.'

'My mum?'

'Look at them.'

Max watched as her mum and Linden's dad laughed together as if they were old friends. Her mum sometimes had this way of laughing that seemed fake, but tonight it sounded as though she was really having a good time.

Max nestled back into the sofa and yawned. 'I guess a good spy mission can bring out the best in anyone.'

Linden watched as Max's mum laughed again and his dad lit up with a warm smile he hadn't seen in a long time. 'I almost forgot he could be like this. He's been so sad these last few years, and now he looks like he used to, like when he was with Mum.'

Linden stopped and stared at his plate. 'Max?' His face flushed and he couldn't look at her. 'I know we've only known each other for a little while, but I feel like we've been friends forever and I can't imagine what life would be like without you.' He paused. 'You're not really going to leave Spy Force, are you? We're a good team, you heard what Harrison said. We shouldn't take that for granted. I don't want to be a spy without you. You really are special and I just wanted to say, well, that I . . .'

Linden inched around to see Max's face and smiled. She was asleep. Snuggled into the side of the sofa, the ribbon from her Spy Force medallion only just visible around her neck. 'Maybe I'll tell you another time.'

He took her plate from her lap as Max inhaled a deep sigh beside him. 'Linden,' she mumbled quietly in her sleep. 'Harrison's in danger. We have to save him. Steinberger. Dretch. Alex . . .'

Linden smiled. Somehow he knew Max would be back at Spy Force.

When Deborah Abela was a small child, she spent most of her time imagining she was on great adventures all over the world. When she grew older, she bought a backpack and a plane ticket and actually went on them. After three years she came home and worked for seven years on one of Australia's most popular children's TV programmes, before leaving to write novels about a small girl who goes on lots of adventures all over the world.

Deborah grew up in Merrylands, a western suburb of Sydney, but now lives in inner-city Glebe with her partner Todd, who is almost as nice as Linden.

Photograph by Todd Decker

MAX REMY
SPY FORCE
BLUE'S
REVENGE